EVERYTHING I OWN

First Fictions Series 3

**Canada Council
for the Arts**   **Conseil des Arts
du Canada**

**ONTARIO ARTS COUNCIL
CONSEIL DES ARTS DE L'ONTARIO**

Guernica Editions Inc. acknowledges the support of the Canada Council
for the Arts and the Ontario Arts Council.
The Ontario Arts Council is an agency of the Government of Ontario.

to Nicole + Emile.
who might recognize
Québec in this
love story

Raymond
10/12/2011

RAYMOND BEAUCHEMIN

EVERYTHING I OWN

GUERNICA
TORONTO • BUFFALO • BERKELEY • LANCASTER (U.K.)
2011

Michael Mirolla, series editor
Lindsay Brown, editor
David Moratto, interior book designer
Guernica Editions Inc.
P.O. Box 117, Station P, Toronto (ON), Canada M5S 2S6
2250 Military Road, Tonawanda, N.Y. 14150-6000 U.S.A.

Distributors:
University of Toronto Press Distribution,
5201 Dufferin Street, Toronto (ON), Canada M3H 5T8
Gazelle Book Services, White Cross Mills, High Town, Lancaster LA1 4XS U.K.
Small Press Distribution, 1341 Seventh St., Berkeley, CA 94710-1409 U.S.A.

First Edition.
Printed in Canada.

Legal Deposit — Fourth Quarter
Library of Congress Catalog Card Number: 2011925254
Library and Archives Canada Cataloguing in Publication
Beauchemin, Raymond, 1962-
Everything I own / Raymond Beauchemin.
(First fictions series ; 3)
ISBN 978-1-55071-346-6
I. Title. II. Series: First fictions series (Toronto, Ont.) ; 3
PS8603.E3631E84 2011   C813'.6   C2011-902184-6

Contents

To Denise
with thanks to Michel Gagnon, Linda Kay
and Carolyn Souaid

There is first of all the problem of the opening, namely, how to get us from where we are, which is, as yet, nowhere, to the far bank. It is a simple bridging problem, a problem of knocking together a bridge. People solve such problems every day. They solve them, and having solved them push on.

— J.M. Coetzee, "Elizabeth Costello"

Je n'ai pas aimé mon père, mais j'ai un père. Et j'en suis heureux.

— Gil Courtemanche, "Un Bon Mort"

Verse One

Beaupré

Whenever Bijou and I were on tour abroad, or flew to France for a holiday with Laurence, my mother would say she was holding the plane up with her hands. I always liked that image: strong, caring, maternal hands under the belly of the plane, bridging a family of three between airports with no more effort than a woman carrying a *soupière* from stove to table. I have felt those hands — my mother's, and my grandmother's, too, I suspect — at other times as well, such as the turbulent patches of my marriage with Bijou. And certainly they got me through my childhood. They bore me up in my attempts at a relationship with my father, even though I had thought, in the ego of youth, I had supported myself with my own hands.

Now it was my turn to hold the plane. Laurence was flying home after 10 years away. I hadn't yet told Bijou. It was Laurence's idea, not to tell her. "*Une surprise*," she said. "He's two."

It's hard to sustain the appearance of calm necessary for a surprise. That morning I had had to invent an errand on top of a real one on Papineau and manufacture a fake time at which that fake errand needed to be accomplished.

"Misha, why can't you go later, *cet après-midi peut-être*?" Bijou asked. "You could drop me off at the studio on the way."

"I'd really rather get it over with now and then come back and get some writing done," I said, which was the truest part of what I had said. I knew she would understand my desire for time to write. "I'm working on a bridge."

"Mmmm. And you have a hard time with bridges, I know. Do you want me to listen to it?" She was seated in the breakfast nook. The sun was turning its attention elsewhere.

I picked my watch up from the kitchen counter. "I better go. Soon. I promise. I just have some tweaking."

"Your tweaking is Plamondon's rewriting. *Prends le tunnel*. The Jacques Cartier is backed up this time of day."

"The tunnel's too far east."

We kissed and I was out the door.

The tunnel wasn't too far east. I just don't like to use it. There are several ways to get to Montreal. Other than someone's hands conveying a plane into a graceful descent into Pierre Elliott Trudeau airport, only one of those modes is not a bridge, and that would be the Tunnel Louis-Hippolyte Lafontaine. I have never been able to figure out exactly how one constructs a tunnel underwater. "It's an immersed tube," my father had once tried to explain. "The pieces are constructed elsewhere, brought to the site, submerged and welded and then ..." I had found myself immersed in incomprehension, submerged in boredom, my ears welded shut. Louis-Hippolyte is to be avoided. If I ever had need to be in Rivière-des-Prairies and I were on Highway 20, I would drive out of my way to go over the Jacques Cartier, north through all the city traffic, to arrive at my destination having avoided the tunnel beneath the St. Lawrence.

Only a bridge will do to cross into Montreal from the South Shore. Each beautiful in its own way, the spans are umbilical cords that tie the region to the belly of Montreal. The Jacques Cartier, the Victoria, the Champlain and the Honoré-Mercier remind residents of towns from

Longueuil to Châteauguay how completely dependent they are on the mother island. No matter how much commuters complain about traffic snarls and daily delays.

I remember one crossing with Bijou over the Champlain. It was after dark, one Sunday in August of 1995, and we were returning from a week, just the two of us, in Wellfleet on Cape Cod. We were late coming over the border so didn't stop at home; instead, we decided to drive straight to the Spectrum to see Paul again. Crossing the Champlain late at night, any night, if the sky is clear, reveals the most spectacular welcome mat: the skyline hugging the river, the skyscrapers of downtown mirroring the height and scale and form of the mountain behind them, the light above Place Ville-Marie a new Pharos guiding wayfarers home, and above all, the lighted cross at the top of Mount Royal, the sign for so many years of Montrealers' true home and the way there.

That night traffic was moderate, enough to slow us down to 50 klicks. Had it been any faster perhaps we would have concentrated on driving one-ten over the bridge and missed our reception, the finale of a fireworks show over La Ronde, gargantuan exploding bouquets of chrysanthemums of red and blue that silhouetted the majestic Jacques Cartier Bridge, followed by green shell-burst rockets and silver tails, golden comets rising and rising and breaking apart into yellow and green pearls.

Whenever I cross the Champlain toward the city at night in the summer, I look to my right, downstream, and hope I might be treated to another detonation of brilliant hues. But such an occurrence, like the week in Wellfleet, like much in life that is beautiful, is fleeting and rare.

But not impossible to duplicate. It happened one more time, while crossing the Mercier. Cresting at 33 metres, on the part of the span that crosses over the St. Lawrence Seaway, Bijou and I saw, beyond the roofs of the houses of LaSalle, the little Eiffel Towers on top of the silhouetted Jacques Cartier Bridge and the golden bursts behind it. This produced in both of us — other than the requisite oooh and ahhhh — the memory of the August crossing over the St. Lawrence, the week on the beach, the emptiness in our guts that had led to our needing Wellfleet.

Looking up through the span's girders now, I could see the 10-foot Eiffel Towers. They didn't usually make me think of the Tower itself, but this morning — just a flash — I saw camera lights and the stage lights of the Théâtre de Paris and heard the echo of the ovation Bijou received for "Quand les hommes vivront d'amour." That was 1988. I neared the centre span, and congratulated myself on the decision to take the bridge instead of the tunnel that morning. And then traffic stopped.

No one's hands held up the car. Nevertheless, I felt suspended, mid-errand, mid-voyage, mid-thought. I put the car in neutral and took my foot off the clutch. I kept the other on the brake and my hand on the stick shift, ready to engage. But there was no movement. I looked in my rear-view mirror at the car behind me, a mustachi-oed man looking in his own mirror. To my right, I could see a half-dozen cars; to my left, another. Behind us were a yellow school bus, a delivery truck and a line of vans, sedans, utility vehicles and rustboxes stretching to just-past dawn. We were mothers and fathers, working men and women, retirees and blue hairs, students and just about anyone who could afford a car, a panoply parked under the canopy of the cantilevered bridge. There is nothing so democratic as a traffic tie-up. I turned on the radio.

For a while, on CHOM, Montreal's reputed rock station, there had been a woman giving traffic reports in a bedroom-y Australian accent. I searched but couldn't find her. Instead, I settled on one of the AM channels, early in the dial, that promised traffic on the "tens." It was coming on 10 after the hour and when it arrived, the report told me nothing I didn't know: traffic heavy on the Jacques Cartier Bridge. I hung around for the weather. I let go the clutch and the brakes, engaged the handbrake. How many times had I performed this same ritual? I'd learned to drive a stick on my own, on a 1983 Nissan Sentra. Bought with money saved from my first major royalties. Thank God, my father hadn't been the teacher, though he had taken me out for my first driving lesson, in our '64 Fairlane. I was 16; the car, 14. We'd grown up together, but by then it was near death. Every hundred he spent on it my father swore was his last.

That first time out, I'd run my hands around the thin, large wheel in front of me. The plastic that faced me was smooth; where my hands curled around it were bumps like grooves for my fingers. I turned, put my arm over the back seat as I had seen my father do, pressed my foot against the accelerator and got a stern "put the car in reverse first." I started over again, went through the remainder of my routine and tapped the gas pedal. We jerked backward and stopped.

"You have to keep your foot on the gas. Stop before you get out of the driveway and check there aren't any cars coming down the street. Check both ends of the street. *Maudit saint-sacrifice de la messe!*"

I drove for about half an hour that morning. I completed the kind of full stops at stop signs that only beginning drivers perform, and managed to annoy plenty of other drivers in the process. The most irritated was the man in the passenger seat. My mother taught me from then on.

I looked upstream over the hood of the car to my left. The skyline was compact and the mountain condensed, not stretched catlike and sleepily behind the city the way it looks from the Champlain. Hochelaga huddled as if its sides were squeezed together. In the winter, I could imagine the city scrunching its shoulders and its gloved hands vigorously rubbing the upper arms of the towers. Below the bridge were parts of the city that the tower residents forgot: the brick duplexes and triplexes with wooden balconies, rough-mown lawns patchy with sand, dotted with hundred-dollar barbecues and plastic three-wheelers whose primary colours were as faded as the memory of which of five kids had first gotten the trike. Yet in this part of the city, below this bridge, were spent the whole lives of men and women. Seventy-year-olds coming out of retirement to drive taxis from the stand outside the Papineau métro because their pension wasn't cutting it. Sixty-year-old matrons wearing curlers at kitchen tables thumbing through classified ads for a car under six grand. Fifty-somethings checking the Gaz Métropolitain meters and remembering to get a 6/49 at lunch. Thousands of people living decades of lives while I watched steam — the single plume of steam in the entire diaphanous vault above the city — rise from the Molson plant.

Beyond the Molson tower and the Radio-Canada building, the clouds seemed suspended, bleached puffs destined for Europe but taking a breather over Montreal, 10 minutes before hooking onto a wind stream for the long trek overseas, where they would pick up yet more moisture. The air was cool that morning, that last day of summer. The weather report predicted mid- to high-teens, which was just fine with me. The weather this time of year is, by nature, unpredictable. It doesn't know how desperately it wants to hang onto summer or how longingly it wishes to fall into autumn. I am not troubled by this unknowingness, or indecision; I think I might prefer it to the fail-safe weather patterns of tropical Africa or Asia where it's either heat or rain, or the southwestern United States, where it's a perfectly dry 40 degrees all summer and a perfectly dry 20 degrees all winter. I was born in New England, in western Massachusetts, where, it was said, "If you don't like the weather, wait five minutes." I had thought this original, and funny, when I first heard it. Then I discovered the same was said of Connecticut, New Hampshire, Maine, Ontario, Quebec, Montreal and probably northwestern Nebraska. I pressed a lever, and my window went down and allowed in the cool air, dampened by the St. Lawrence River below me.

I pushed a button of the radio to switch bands back to FM and yet another to scan for a station. Morning radio is so filled with chatter it should all be called talk radio. I hit the button several times before the scan function stopped and I found myself crossing another bridge. Bijou was on the radio.

———

I ran up the three worn wooden stairs, paused briefly on the porch and waved to my left toward the kitchen door where I knew Madame Truffaut would be watching. I skipped down the next three stairs, turned and headed down the longer flight toward the basement. I crashed through the door, which slammed against Marc's dad's workbench.

"*Hé, les gars*! You gotta hear this!" I said.

We five, sixth-graders at l'Ecole Maisonneuve, were the Hit-masters, the Little Rockers (styled after Pagliaro's Rockers), Hochelaga-Maisonneuve, the Retro-Francos, Live au Spectrum. Our name changed with every gust of the cultural wind. We were the Olympix in anticipation of the Games, and Métro when they began extending the Green Line. For a time, we saw ourselves on the road to success as the Bonaventures, and then Ville Marie (but that lasted a week at most, when Madame Truffaut forced us to include Marc's little sister Marie).

"Where've you been?" Marc was turned toward me, from where he stood in the centre of the room. There was a bare light bulb over the wooden workbench and another at the bottom of the staircase that led directly upstairs into the Truffauts' living room. The effect was to backlight Marc.

I walked out of the shadow and into the room, shrugged out of my parka. Above Marc, tied to one of the numerous pipes — hot water, cold water, waste water — was a kitchen cord. Dangling from the other end of the cord was a used paper-towel roll with an almost hairless tennis ball duct-taped to it. Marc was to the right of our mic, Richard to the left, with a 10-dollar guitar. Jim was sprawled on the chesterfield reading a list of albums in a newspaper ad hawking 12 LPs for 99 cents. Norman leaned on the back two legs of a creaky wooden Windsor. One of the pipes pinged in the cold.

Norman sat forward, letting his weight slam the front legs of the chair down. The portable record player shook, and the needle slid across "Smokin' in the Boys' Room."

"Nice move, nitwit," Jim said.

Norman backslapped Jim's foot. Jim kicked back.

"Where were you?" Marc asked again. "We had to start without you."

"What do you have?" Richard asked. He put the guitar down on the arm of the couch. Jim dropped his paper, reached behind his head and laid the guitar across his chest. He plucked at its plastic strings.

I lifted up the Sam the Record Man bag to show them. Inside was a brand spanking new 45 from Terry Jacks that I'd heard in the store and bought. "This is amazing. It's a song about a guy who's dying and he's saying good-bye to his friend and his father and his wife. 'We had joy, we had fun, we had seasons in the sun.' You gotta hear it." I reached into the bag to take out the disc.

Marc grabbed the bag. "I said, 'Where were you?' "

"Hey, man, what gives?"

"We had a practice at five o'clock after my paper route and you weren't here," he said.

"So what?"

Richard said, "So Marc had to take lead vocals and you know he sounds like a horse."

Marc took a swipe at Richard with the bag.

"Hey! That's my record!" I said and reached for it.

Marc put it behind his back.

"My mother made me go down to the Bay with her, then I begged her to let me go to Sam's. Is that what you wanted to know?"

"*Menteur.*"

"What?"

"*Maudit menteur.*"

I shoved him. He fell back, arms splayed out, and dropped the bag. I jumped on him. "Take it back, dirt-bag."

Before he could, the boys had yanked me up by the arms.

"What you have to call him that for?" Jim said.

" 'Cause he is."

"Prove it," I said.

"Marie!" Marc shouted.

We heard the scrape of a chair along the kitchen floor and the shuffle of his sister's feet. The door to the basement opened. "*Qu'est-ce que tu veux?*"

"Marie, where did you go after school today?"

"I was downtown with Marie-Michèle."

"And how did you get there?"

"*L'autobus jusqu'à Frontenac et puis après ça en métro.*"

"And did you see anyone on the métro?"

I felt my face warming. I hadn't seen little Marie Truffaut on the crowded train. Nor her friend, Marie-Michèle, whom I knew by sight because she was almost always over at the house. So I'd been caught out in a little lie, *une menterie.*

"Michel was there. He was with Louise Pelletier. I saw them holding hands."

"*Merci, Marie. C'est tout.*"

"Screw you, Marc."

"*Non, non*, Michel. I think you are the one who is screwed," Marc said.

"He's the one who's screwing, you mean," Norman said.

"I am not," I said.

"Wouldn't even know how," Marc said.

"Screw you," I said again.

"Let's hear the record," Richard said. He picked it up off the floor, gently shook it out of its paper sleeve.

"I'm confused," Norman said after the first listen. "If this guy's dying how did he make the record?"

"Whaddya mean, 'if this guy's dying'? He's not the one dying," I said.

"Well then who is?" he asked.

From the couch, speaking into the air above him, Jim said: "The singer musta known ahead he was going to die and then just wrote and recorded the song."

"The singer's not talking about his own life," I said. "The singer's not even the guy who wrote it. It's by someone named Brel. It's not this guy Jacks who wrote it. He just sang it. Brel wrote it. And someone —" I looked at the record label "— named McKuen. He must be the translator."

"Then who's Terry Jacks?" Jim asked.

"The singer, you twit," Richard said.

"Canadian," Marc said, in a tone that meant English Canadian.

"What does it matter?" I said. "The songwriter's Belgian and the English lyrics are by someone else."

"Probably an American, from *les états tout-nus*," Marc said.

I didn't know which crime I wanted to smack him for — being an idiot or being right about American influence. CHOM was running an ad — "It's music ... and more:

L'Esprit de Montréal" with more than a dozen singers' photographs and not one of them Canadian. And CJFM highlighted artists for an hour every night. But only the big ones, the Brits and the Americans. And this was three years after all radio stations were supposed to be playing more Canadian content.

"Richard, play the song," I said, annoyed, impatient, not even sure if I wanted to hear it again with Marc the bozo.

We listened to it I don't know how many times, Marc fading in and out of attention, until from "Goodbye to you, my trusted friend," we had the lyrics memorized. When we had it down, I stood up in front of the mic; Richard stood opposite me with his guitar; Jim kept time slapping his thighs, pursing his lips and letting out an airy "tsssh" for the high-hats and Norman moved the needle back to the beginning of the song. Marc sat on a stool by the workbench, where he mimed his "piano." We knew no better than this: the two of us who could sing, the two who hung around because they were never picked to play hockey or baseball, the last whose mother preferred he invited his friends over rather than hang out in the streets the way his older brother had — "and look where that landed him," she told her second son. We knew no better than the cheap make-believe and free dreams of Montreal's working-class.

"I don't think the guy's dying," Jim said, still on his back. "I think he's committing suicide."

"How can you tell?" Richard said. He held his guitar by the neck.

"It's like a suicide note," Jim said. "He's telling everyone goodbye."

"And how do you know it's his wife at the end?" Norman said. "He says 'my little one.' It could be he's got a daughter named Michelle." He sat back in the chair, letting it lean against the exposed brick wall.

"Yeah, I don't think he's married," Richard said. "He's talking to his friend in the first verse about looking at all the girls. ... But then how does he have a daughter?"

"You don't have to be married to have a kid, idiot," Marc said, as he slid off his stool.

"Screw you," Richard said.

"Oh, not this again," I said.

"And he says, 'It's hard to die,' so I don't know if he's killing himself," Jim said, and sat up as if to punctuate his thoughts. "I think he's just dying."

"You just said you thought it was suicide," I said.

"Yeah, but I just remembered he says, 'It's hard to die'."

"You think it's easy committing suicide?" Norman said. "You can try killing yourself 10 times before you finally do it."

"Oh, give me a break," Marc said. He gave Norman a bit of a shove to the shoulder. The chair fell forward to upright. "What do you know about suicide?"

"I just do, 's all. I don't have to tell you." And a vacancy sign fell over his face.

"Musta been some nitwit, it took him 11 times."

"Marc, *t'es niaiseux*," I said.

"What did I do? I say he's a liar."

"Everyone's a liar to you," I said.

"Well, he did catch you, didn't he?" Richard said.

"K-i-s-s-i-n-g," Jim sang.

I pushed Jim's shoulder.

"Hey, what was that for?" he said.

"I didn't kiss her."

"Oh, so you admit you were with Louise Pelletier!" Richard said.

I shrugged. "So what?"

"She's got big tits," Norman said, exiting momentarily the vacant room in his head.

"So what?!" Marc said.

Jim made a sucking noise from where he was slouched on the couch.

"Oh, shit, man." My watch said 10 minutes to six. My father sat down at the dinner table promptly at a quarter-to and he expected everyone to be there with him.

In the end, which was just the next day, we dropped "Seasons in the Sun" from our repertoire. It wasn't the song's mood — although how depressing could it have been? It was on the charts for months — but the multiple changes in pitch that none of us could successfully pin down.

"It's like the mating call of a walrus," Jim said.

"A walrus screwing a hole in the ice is more like it," Marc said.

"I mean why does he even do it?" Richard asked. "He can barely make the notes."

"He's gotta do it," I said. "It makes it more emotional."

"Emotional or not, we can't figure out whether he's trying to kill himself or just dying, and we don't know if Michelle's his daughter or his girlfriend or his wife," Marc said. "It's just too hard to sing about some shit you don't know what you're singing about. I vote we scratch it."

"All those in favour, say 'aye'," Richard said.

I raised my hand, too. I couldn't reach the notes. It was unanimous.

Norman looked relieved.

I had a new 45 with me.

"What now?" Marc asked. Though it wasn't really a question. "Another American? Oh, I forgot: 'God Is an American'."

"Riffling through your father's Ferland albums again, I see," I said.

He ignored my attempted comeback and dug deeper. "You got some John Denver? 'Sunshine on my shoulders makes me hoo-wee!' How 'bout some Elton John?"

"Who's the nitwit now? Elton John's not American," Jim said. "He's British."

"British, American," Marc said. "It's all the same. It's English."

"Well, these guys aren't English," I said. I took the record from the bag.

"Been to Sam's again," Richard said.

"Not been with Louise again, have you?" Norman asked.

I shrugged. I had been, but that didn't mean I had to tell them. Norman was right. She did have big tits from what I could see, which was the occasional sideways glance when we were in the subway train together. Anyway, what's wrong with being with a girl with big tits? Especially when you're almost 12 and she's your first girlfriend, big tits or not.

"First comes love..." Jim said.

"You're pathetic," I said.

"OK, Lover Man, what have you got this time?" Richard said.

I handed the disc to Norman. He looked at it. "Blue Suede," he said.

"I think they pronounce it Swede. They're Swedish."

"But that doesn't make any sense," Norman said. "Blue Suede makes sense. I mean Swede is like blonde, it's not blue. Suede can be blue, like blue jeans."

"Just put it on," I said.

And there it was. They sat spellbound through the entire two minutes and 51 seconds.

"We finally found a song Marc can sing," Richard said. "Ooga-chaga, ooga-ooga-ooga-chaga."

"Funny," he said.

"I love it!" Jim said. "What a great intro. It's so cool. And singing the first verse over it, with no music, just letting the background vocals be the beat, man, that's so cool. And the first musical instrument you hear's my part."

"Thought you'd like that," I said.

"Horns, though," Norm said. "We don't have horns."

"You can be the horns," I said.

"I can't be the horns. I don't know how to be the horns."

"Do like we all do," I said. "Make it up."

"I don't know," Marc said. "*C'a l'air nègre.*"

"What did you say?"

"You heard me. I think they sound black."

"They are not," I said. "They're from Sweden."

It was the lousiest, but perhaps best defense this about-to-be-12-year-old could come up with. It didn't seem right what Marc had said, but neither did my response. "Hooked on a Feeling" got one listen in the Truffauts' basement. Which was one more listen than Elton John's "Bennie and the Jets," the Jackson Five's "Dancing Machine" and "The Show Must Go On" from Three Dog

Night, rejected, by Marc, for being British, American or black. "Band on the Run" we listened to, and liked, even after the hours of debate over whether the lyrics were a post-Beatle code of some sort. But we couldn't wrap our fake instruments around the ornate instrumentation that bridged the three segments of the song. As school ended, Gordon Lightfoot — who Marc recognized as from Ontario and therefore worthy of only scant attention — came out with "Sundown."

"This is gonna hit number one," I said. "In the U.S., you watch."

"Who cares if it hits number one in the U.S.?" Marc said. "Why don't you stop thinking like an American?"

Like my response to his attack on blacks, I didn't know how to answer. Why was my being an American so offensive? Did my French sound so different from his? And how could I "think like an American" when I'd spent more than half my life in Quebec? All I was saying was the song was going to be big, way bigger than just Canada. Why didn't he get that?

"Give me the record back," I said. "Go back to listening to René Simard."

Marc made for me, but Jim stopped him.

Norman took the disc off the record player.

"Oh, yeah, I forgot," I said. "You're more of a *Bouts d'choux* fan."

He leaped at me, but I was gone.

I left for Louise's house.

And there's where I spent the summer of my 13th year.

Louise had an older sister with a record player and a collection of records — singles and long-players — which we listened to when she wasn't around. Louise and I sat side by side on the floor at the foot of her sister's bed. We listened to the albums over and over, the way I had with *les gars*, but without the taped-up tennis ball and the knee-slap drum kit. When an album side was over, Louise would get up and walk over to the dresser on which the stereo turntable sat. She was tall, all legs, with denim cutoffs whose white, frayed ends contrasted against the deep, smooth darkness of her tan. I would look at her ankles and calves, the turn-down and flattening at the back of the knee, then follow the hamstring up the back of the thigh and think/sing to myself, "I feel like makin' love." I couldn't keep my eyes off those legs, her shapely back and the waist tie of her halter top, which was always a variation on yellow. She wore tops of dandelion, straw, gold, canary and lemon, colours of summer, colours of youthful pleasure, perky smiling colours. She kept her hair, brown in the winter but sun-bleached in summer to near-blonde perfection, tied up with yellow fabric that matched her top. On her nape, downy blonde hair.

It was the summer of Bachman Turner Overdrive and Robert Charlebois, Mahogany Rush and Harmonium. When she flipped the record over and replaced the needle, she would turn with a smile, wide and open, an invitation. Yeah, she had big tits, but it was her smile that drew all the attention. It was her smile that said "c'mon over." It was her smile that said "what do you want to do next?" Then she would fold herself into a seat by my side and gently nod her head to the beat, her lips a pale rose, folded around the words, and her hand would settle itself in mine. It was the summer of "Annie's Song," and "Please Come to Boston," Steely Dan, Joni Mitchell and Eric Clapton. Of summer nights and endless calls to the CKVL all-request line. It was my summer of love.

"My father wants to know who this boy is that's been hanging around the house all summer," Louise said one afternoon. We were walking along Hochelaga Street. There were heavy trucks everywhere carrying dirt away or hauling material to the site of the new stadium. The city was two years away from hosting the Games. My father said they'd never be ready: "The most they've been able to do is come up with a stupid logo."

Louise and I were looking for a *dépanneur* to buy ice cream.

"Your sister has a boyfriend?"

"Silly. He means you. He wants to meet you."

"Have I really been hanging around that much?"

She gave me a bump with her elbow.

"They've got a good soft-serve here," I said.

"My friends are wondering where I've been all summer," Louise said.

I ordered for us and paid from my allowance.

"You haven't gone anywhere. You've been here."

"I asked my mother if I could invite another friend."

"Great idea."

"You could invite Marc."

"Marc? Why would I invite Marc? He's a jerk, always talking down about me being American. I'm just as Canadian as he is."

"You could still invite him."

I shrugged.

"Josée's coming. She likes him."

"Tell her he's a jerk."

"She thinks he's cute."

There was a bench under the front window of the corner store. We sat. In the window were posters for Molson Export and Export A and a sign announcing that the next drawing for the *Loterie Olympique* Canada — one million dollars! who had ever heard of such a thing? — was July 16th. I slouched back with my legs stretched out onto the sidewalk and she sat crossed-legged facing me. I licked my ice cream, bit into the wafer cup. Louise was so close I could feel the coolness of her vanilla breath, could sense the up and down motion of her breasts, held in so tentatively by her butter-coloured top, could see the way her lips formed what she was saying and then how they would stop, part, open in a slight oval, and her tongue pierced the opening just as, in perfect timing, she lifted the cone to her mouth.

And yet, and yet and yet and yet, despite a summer of holding hands, singing to records, remembering lyrics and letting them spill out of our memories to make room for the next, swimming at the public pool, lying head to head on towels kept warm by the sun-drenched concrete and walking around the neighbourhood in the dusky post-dinner light, I began to feel she didn't know me. I couldn't invite Marc. She must have known that. I'd told her what had happened to us that day, and how I felt he'd become so weird, saying those things about black people and Americans. I thought she understood why I couldn't invite him and yet, there she was. "You could still invite him."

Every time I heard Marc's voice in my head I heard the words "*nègre*" and "*états tout-nus*" and when I heard these words, I felt empty inside. This wasn't a feeling I wanted. I had what I wanted. I had left Marc's house that buggy June day and sought out what I wanted. And here Louise was asking me to cross that chasm and meet up with Marc again, while the only thing I wanted to ford was the space between Louise and me. I wished to close up the expanse before it grew any wider. I could feel her. I knew where in the space beside me her breasts were, her shoulders and arms, her face, eyes, ears, nose and lips. I turned, abruptly, toward her, leaned in and planted a kiss on her cool, ice-cream-wet lips. The kiss, as brief as it was, lingered. I could taste it. I was sure she could, too. I licked my bottom lip. Our first kiss tasted of her, of vanilla. I smiled. She smiled.

"I don't want Marc to come," I said.

"*Je comprends*," she said.

There. I had connected.

We finished our cones.

That weekend, we trundled north to a lake unfamiliar to me, near St. Adolphe. When my family vacationed, it was back to the Richelieu Valley *pour faire les foins*. My grandfather counted on my father's help to bring in the hay every summer. He owned 50 acres, enough for 5,000 bales of hay, enough for the animals he kept on a further 20, enough to keep me busy for a couple of weeks every summer after I'd turned 10 and was considered big enough to help. Grandpapa drove the Massey-Ferguson. Scratch the mud off and you could perhaps make out the sunburned pink of its youth. My father and his brothers worked the baling machine, and I and one of my father's uncles followed in another trailer, pulled by a tractor driven by yet another great-uncle, picking up the bales and heaving those *bottes* into piles. The work began early in the morning, as soon as the dew had dried, and we worked until dusk when the dust of the land coated our throats, our eyes, our nostrils, and the grass itself — timothy, with its corn-dog-like tops, and spindly branched alfalfa — caused us to itch in every other crevice.

It was understood when I asked my father and mother permission to go with the Pelletiers to the lake in St. Adolphe that I would not be out late Saturday, that I would be up at the crack of the first bell Sunday morning and ready for church. Immediately after mass we were off to Sabrevois. Whoever wrote the commandment about keeping the Sabbath holy had clearly spent too much time wandering the desert and no time working land. The hay was ready when the hay said it was ready and it was up to the farmer to answer its call. "You need three days straight, no rain," my father said. "This is it." The work would continue until we were finished and every eye-stinging, nose-scratchy, twine-tied bale was stacked in the loft of the barn. Then when the grass was ready for a second cutting, we'd do it again.

I don't remember much of the ride, *monsieur ou madame* Pelletier, or the lake. In fact, I can say I recall only one thing: Beaupré. And when I remember it now, even sitting in my car on Jacques Cartier Bridge, it is hard to separate the memory of that day — the ride, the parents, the swim, lunch — from all that came afterward. Beaupré is as preserved in my memory as the time out of which it arose even though that time has passed like ice melt in the St. Lawrence. So much is wrapped around that memory now that, although I can recall it, I cannot retrieve it unaccompanied by the years of associated recollections that followed. My memory of Beaupré is like a stalk of hay plucked from the bale of my 43 years. I've picked this one, because, parked on the Jacques Cartier Bridge, I happened to hear Bijou on the radio. But, any fragment from that fertile ground of *souvenirs* could have come from hearing that song. For everything was Beaupré — and Beaupré, its sum, its parts — was everything. I cannot imagine how my life would have been different without Beaupré because I have not lived a life without it.

I have a friend who is a lifelong disciple of Bruce Springsteen. He can remember the exact night in August 1975 when he dropped a quarter in the Wurlitzer at the pizzeria down the street and accidentally punched in the number-letter combination for "Born To Run." He remembers he was with a friend J-P and another, André. He had two slices. Oil collected like puddles in the little discs of pepperoni. The meatballs were small, dry and peppery. He had a white T-shirt silk-screened with the cover of the Eagles' "One of These Nights." What he'd thought he had on the jukebox was Steppenwolf's "Born To Be Wild." J-P sneered at this new song, whatever it was. André was noncommittal. My friend Pierre said hearing that song for the first time took him down a road from which he's never returned. He remembers his reaction to that first time even though he has heard the song on a thousand occasions since and has had as many reactions to it.

And as it is with Beaupré so it is with Bijou.

I spent most of that Saturday at the lake — my own Lac Louise — trying to recapture the moment Louise and I had shared on the bench in front of the *dépanneur* on Hochelaga Street. Just one more kiss, that's all I wanted. Toward the end of the day, after we were called in from the lakefront to wash and prepare for dinner, I got what I wanted.

Louise was on a dumpy old cottage-style sleeper couch drying her hair with a towel when I walked into the room. The lace curtain was drawn on the large window right-angled to where Louise sat, in a suffusion of late-afternoon sunlight. I closed the door quietly and went directly to the couch, where I sat next to her. The towel was damp and soft and smelled woodsy, having been dried outside on the line. I put my index finger to her lips to quiet her and leaned toward her. Our lips grazed each other and I backed away slowly. She was smiling. I kissed her again, and felt her lips part. Mine opened to receive her darting tongue, sweet and tangy as homemade lemonade. We kissed like this for a long time. I touched the lemon-hued top of her bathing suit, and fingered the edge of it, the line of the strap, followed the seam to where the strap connected with the cup. I traced a circle around her nipple. My hand, open, lifted her breast and I felt the endlessness of opportunity.

Then the door opened.

"*Le souper est presq*—Louise!" Denise, her sister, gasped.

I backed off quickly, plunked down on my side of the couch.

"What were you doing?" she asked.

I assumed the question was directed at me. "I was reaching around Louise to ... to get the magazine there," I said, and pointed to the stack on Louise's right.

Denise stood in the opening she'd created, quietly, probably trying to decipher how much of what I had said she wanted to believe. I projected the most sincere smile

I could, but was sure it wasn't enough. Denise looked at me, at the magazine, Louise. She advanced, grabbed the magazine. "Beaupré," she said. "*Tu les connais?*"

"*Non, c'est un groupe Montréalais?*"

"From around." She handed me the magazine.

The guys in the band — who I would later know as the two Marcels, Pierre and 'Ti Gus — wore white wide-collared shirts with sleeves whose cuffs puffed out like chefs' toques, and bell-bottomed blue jeans. The lone woman in the group was the focal point of the photograph. She had her arms around the two men nearest her and leaned forward a bit, laughing; her blonde hair long and unruly. Her jeans were white as January in Chibougamau and her blouse blue. She was the only one with eyes straight at the camera. Everyone else was looking at her or the other guys. They were all mugging, they had been having a good time. Nationalism is sexy! the photo said. It's youthful! Invigorating! Fun! "*Hé, tout l'monde; il y a une chanson qu'on chante*: C'mon, get 'appy!" Thirty-odd years and two referendums later, I know this was the message behind the image. Back then, I was focused on the woman's partly unbuttoned blouse, just a *soupçon* of breast behind the thin veil of *fleurdelisé* blue.

Her name, the magazine said, was Bijou.

I hadn't owned an actual album to that point. I'd only ever bought singles. Whether it was the fault of my meagre allowance or the fact that I was an integral part of the target audience of the radio market and therefore programmed ("Don't touch that dial!") to the *terra cognita* of Top 10, a world of one-hit wonders, supergroups, girl groups, boy bands, made-for-TV bubblegum groups, singer-songwriters, pop stars, rock stars and teen idols,

I was the kid who purchased whatever was popular at that moment. I lived for the charts. Every Saturday night, I was by the radio, either the kitchen AM/FM or the transistor I'd gotten for Christmas the previous year with a little jack for an earphone. ("What's he doing up there?" I could hear my father ask. "Listening to music," my mother answered. He scoffed. "Music," he said. "If he doesn't finish his work, I'll give him a pounding so hard he'll hear music in his head for a month.") On Mondays after school I went downtown and picked up the printed version of the *Radio-Mutuel* hot sellers and checked out Sam the Record Man's own list of best-selling singles. Then I scanned the rack of 45s to see what I was missing.

The 45s always took pride of place at the front of the store near the cash register, making it a place of congregation, and the best spot for whoever worked the cash to keep an eye on nimble fingers. The album bins were in long aisles that took up most of the store, placed alphabetically by group. Every once in a while I would venture into the bin area, like Cartier streaming up the St. Lawrence toward Hochelaga and the discovery that would change his life. I knew albums existed in the way explorers knew the Orient and India existed. I knew groups recorded singles and collected them into albums and, generally, the best thing on the album was the single — which I already owned for one-tenth the price. I also knew, after that summer listening to Denise Pelletier's albums with her sister, Louise, that some artists preferred to create albums, which were more spherical in conceit and concept. They were projects, full-framed houses; rounded-out thoughts, like whole worlds onto themselves, each song a landing point from which to take off to the next tune. Albums were, that summer of discovery, my *terres neuves*. Yet, until Beaupré, I'd found no reason to buy one, to risk the four bucks.

And, then, one August Monday, the last Monday before *la rentrée*, I had nine good reasons for dropping hard-earned coin. Four came off Side 1: *La Complainte d'un chien sur la rue Frontenac, Export, Le Vrai Secret du bonheur, Chasseur de rêves.* And the remainder were from Side 2 : *Le Feu des origines, Le Soleil à midi, Dimanche on verra, Visite chez Madame Hébert,* and *Objet d'art.*

I also had five (though, more truthfully, one) reason to buy the self-titled debut album of Beaupré, whose members hailed from Montreal, *et les environs*, and not from Ste. Anne de Beaupré at all. The one reason was the woman on the cover of the magazine. And there she was again, in my hands, with her four compatriots, silhouetted in a way and superimposed on a new background, a blue-tinged old photograph of Frontenac Street in winter, piled snow masking the makes and models of buried cars, snow mounded on balconies and stairways, snow waiting to be removed from sidewalks, early-morning snow, no-two-flakes-are-the-same snow, sugar snow. The band members weren't sharing an in-joke the way they had been on the magazine. They were somewhat serious, unsmiling but for one whose lip turned up slightly in challenge. Positioned in front of the winter street scene, one guy with his arms crossed, one with his arms around the two men closest to him, a scarf draped casually around his neck, she close but separate, they were more statement than question, more declaration than invitation. She was also featured in the photograph on the back of the album, the blonde hair shorter, seated next to a harp, the guys around her, three to the right, one to the left so as not to be obstructed by the harp, all the men with traditional-looking Québécois instruments. Under the photo, the caption read: *Beaupré est: Marcel Royal (guitare acoustique, voix), Marcel Beaupré (guitares acoustique et électrique, accordéon, voix), Pierre Lapierre (basse), Bijou Boisclair (clavier, harpe, voix), et Auguste "Ti Gus" Forêt (batterie et percussions).* These then were the five reasons, but I didn't know that until I played the album.

It is impossible to separate my initial impression of Beaupré from what came afterward, as impossible as it is to separate lyric from music or voice from lyric. Even now, when I hear a song develop in my head, I hear not just lyric or music, but both, a married couple, two hearts, one flesh. We hear the words and the music in concert, in unison, not sequentially, and what is voice but the expression of that lyric? I know this is true, as true as my growing up and marrying Bijou. Have you ever been stuck in an elevator and forced to listen to Muzak? If you know the tune, your mind will fill in the lyrics, regardless of whether you know them all. It might simply be the refrain you sing. It may be part of the first verse. Your mind crosses the vale that connects lyric and music.

My young ears couldn't yet separate one part of the music from the other, but I could follow the propulsive command of the lead guitar, could hear the strings apart from the bass. I rolled and tapped and hissed with the drums. The band had a close-fitting sound, snug as their jeans. No instrument or note was wasted. And all of it cried: *"Je suis Québécois."* These were songs about

Chinese *dépanneur* owners; longshoremen in the Old
Port huddled in cigarette smoke while they wait for a
container ship to come in; managers of hotels on Ste.
Catherine St. watching the whores and their johns;
hunters up in the Mauricie; a M'iqmaq in Shefferville
trimming a moccasin with multi-coloured beads the
size of roe; an artist in the Latin Quarter asleep in her
loft. Years from then, when people tried to imagine Quebec, to know it, they might read *Kamouraska* or *L'avalée
des avalés* or *Beautiful Losers*, but they would not know
it any more intimately than by listening to the music of
Beaupré.

I lay on my stomach on the floor of my bedroom, head
propped up with one hand, the other scribbling as fast
as I could the lyrics of the songs on *Beaupré*. I would get
one line down, get up, pick up the arm of the record player and try to place it in the record groove I'd just heard,
then get down again and transcribe the next line. It was
like one of my grade school grammar lessons. Up and
down like that, a three-minute song can take a good 15
minutes. I should've just moved the whole record player
down to the ground; I don't know why I never thought of
that. Still, up and down like that, I managed to get each
song line by line, and later, re-reading my work and singing along with the record these lyrics about Quebec and
Montreal, which I thought I knew so well, and about
Quebecers and Montrealers, whom I also thought I
knew, I began to discover what happens when one word
is bound to another. That spring, I'd had some inkling
Terry Jacks was not singing about his choice to kill himself nor was he singing about some inoperable cancer.
Nor had Jacques Brel written lyrics that were in the least

autobiographical. Yet whatever the source of inspiration, the song elicited feelings of identification, a sense that said, "Yes, that's how I feel." That's why it had charted so high. The musical grammar that Beaupré's main songwriters, Marcel Royal and Marcel Beaupré, taught was as essential to the expression of Québécois culture as the *comptes rendus* and verb conjugations of school.

Perhaps I didn't realize it then — in fact, I am sure it was as unconscious as the dreams of the political and religious revolutionaries of the mid-1960s — but as the album *Beaupré* revolved around the spindle of the record player, I was having my own Quiet Revolution. I was learning and building on the vocabulary of the generation that had pushed, prodded and pulled the province to cut the 400-year-old lanyard tying it to the Church and secure itself to its Québécois soul. I had never understood why they called these stirrings of an independence movement the Quiet Revolution. The generation that shucked off the *soutane* proclaimed its independence quite loudly. We Quebecers were to become captains of our own ship. And when one is captain, he is allowed to haul anchor. Where the Quiet Revolution left a hole in our cultural window, Beaupré — as the most audible and visible expression of what "Quebec" now meant — gave us a new glass through which to see the world and through which the world could see us.

Beaupré's songs gave voice to this feeling — damn Marc! How could he think I was anything but the Quebecer I felt I was?! — and the pride we could and should have in our *fleuve*-deep traditions. Once it was out there on the waves, there was no taking it back, no anchoring it down. And more than that: Beaupré's success legitimized our sentiments and thoughts, made us believe that what we had was worth singing and crowing about. And I swore, with all the zeal of an immigrant — born in Massachusetts, the cradle of U.S. liberty, spoon-fed Revolutionary War pap about taxation without representation and the rights of the people — to be the first communicant in this revolutionary new Québécois church, first ensign aboard this good ship.

So, it was with some *nostalgie* that I heard "Chasseur de rêves" on the radio that morning on the bridge. The story of a hunter off to bag a moose in the Mauricie region who recalls — while an early snow falls quietly around him — his first hunting trip with his dad, dead the last year after a life of hard knocks and hard drunks, its last line was: "*Il était un bon homme.*" The song received a fair bit of airplay on French album-rock stations when it came out in the winter of 1974-75. It was the nectar of Marcel Royal's tenor that made the song as good as it was. Pitched high, his vocal turn projected an almost childlike purity, while Bijou's part — she notched her alto voice down — swirled around Marcel's like ghostly flakes.

> *Dans la forêt, froidure et poudrerie,*
> *Le chasseur s'accroupit avec son fusil;*
> *Les yeux sont vifs, les doigts sont vites,*
> *Mais camouflé dans un arbre, le cœur est endormi.*

What really clinched the song, though, was Marcel Beaupré, whose baritone recalled the roughness of our fathers, their bare, open hands against our backsides, their scratchy post-work cheeks against our lips.

"*C'était une autre époque,*" Bijou had said once in response to a newspaper reporter's query about rumours then floating around — this was in the late-1980s — about the possibility of a Beaupré reunion. "*C'était une autre époque*" was her polite way of saying no.

She'd said the same to me, a few years later, in a different context.

"All I'm saying, Bijou, is there's no reason, on a greatest hits album, not to include songs that are so clearly yours," I said.

"Misha," she said, " 'Fille de Gaspé' and 'Angèle' are beautiful songs. But that was so long ago. I don't even sing them in concert anymore. That was Beaupré. *C'est passé.*"

There was no denying her. For some songs (not all, because there are always exceptions — the genius of genius is that it allows for exceptions), there is no separating music from its time, from its place. "Fille de Gaspé" and "Angèle" were among those songs that broke through the continuum, at least I thought so. They were not tied to issues, were not political, not driven by ideas. They were love songs. But Bijou identified them as of the era of Beaupré, and Bijou had the last word.

And I jump ahead of myself. "Fille de Gaspé" and "Angèle," like "Premier Cri," which Bijou did include on the greatest hits album, were from Beaupré's second album, *Bleu et blanc*. "Premier Cri" was the first song of her own that she'd ever recorded, still an audience favourite after all these years.

I glanced at the clock on the radio. The car hadn't budged, but I still had time to get Laurence.

Verse Two

Le Bleu et le blanc

It was beyond me how the police expected an entire bridge-full of cars, vans, buses, trucks and motorcycles to move over to one side and leave them a lane through which to pass. Yet, in every similar situation in which I have found myself — on the Décarie, on the Met, once in the Ville-Marie Tunnel — it has worked. Drivers make way for police the way a crowd makes way for a star's arrival at a premiere. This time, on the Jacques Cartier, we inched to the right, one vehicle at a time. There was barely enough room, given the narrowness of the shoulder and the tight space between lanes to negotiate. But we did it, and our hard work — minus the shouting and tempers — was dutifully noted on the radio.

"Police have arrived on the Jacques Cartier Bridge," the traffic reporter said. "The cause of the tie-up is not a stalled car as previously reported, but a man who has climbed one of the support beams. Here is Sgt. Maurice St-Émard of the Montreal Police Department."

His voice was that of the practiced spokesperson, calm and assured, yet with a hint he's not quite told all he knows:

"We have a situation on the Jacques Cartier Bridge. Police are arrived. A man drive his car onto the bridge, and when he reach the centre of the bridge, he get out and start to climb a support beam. As I say, the police are arrived and the situation should be clear soon."

I leaned forward and strained to see out my windshield. I couldn't see the bumper of the car in front of me. Not a good sign. The same behind me. If objects are truly closer than they appear in the passenger-side mirror, I wasn't going anywhere. I killed the engine, but kept the power on to listen to the radio. An ambulance, a fire truck, a ladder truck and another pair of police cars pulled up in the newly cleared centre lane. I was now boxed in.

How the jumper got over the fence I had no idea. Shaped like the top of a question mark, the fence — three-quarter-inch square metal rods — rose and curved three metres above the sidewalks on either side of the bridge. Barrier or not, though, a good three to four dozen people, with obviously more imagination than I, try to kill themselves every year on this bridge and about 25 per cent of them succeed. I was surprised the figure wasn't even higher. If someone wants to kill himself, he's going to figure out a way to do it, barrier or not.

It took Norman's uncle 11 tries. How he got over the barrier, I don't know. Perhaps in the summer of 1974 there was no question-mark-shaped fence.

In the summer of 1976, the Olympics fully underway and the city, nation and world held under the sway of Nadia Comaneci, our little gang continued to use the Truffauts' basement as our hangout. Whatever differences I'd had with Marc were forgotten, healed like old hockey bruises. It was the gang's last hurrah together. Our group — Marc's sister called us Les Choristes, a joke of a name for five boys who despite being Catholic couldn't tell a Psalter from a salter — was having its Yoko Ono moment. Richard and his family were moving to Toronto because his father's company had been spooked by the possibility of a win by the Parti Québécois, and Jim was off to an English high school, his parents apparently satisfied he had a decent grounding in French and not wanting to jeopardize a potential future career. He said.

The Christmas after "Seasons in the Sun," my grand-mother, over the strong objection of my father, who'd told her to get me a chemistry set, gave me a six-string acoustic guitar. I played it nonstop, much to the irritation of my father, whose parental perhaps even biological imperative, it seemed, was to quash any attempt at language — musical or spoken (unless spoken to) — on my part. Eventually, I picked out the opening chords of "House of the Rising Sun" and Neil Young's "Old Man." When I went to the Truffauts' basement with the guitar and a copy of Beaupré's album, no one was interested in playing along. The pretend band had disbanded while I was with Louise. The next summer, we did listen, though, to *Bleu et blanc*, Beaupré's new release. Marc congratulated me on finally seeing the light of Québécois culture.

"Finally, you know? Quebec for Quebecers, that's what I'm talking about," Marc said.

"That's your father talking. You don't know what you're talking about."

"Me? Aren't you the one who's nuts over Beaupré? Don't you listen to the words?"

Of course I had. I had memorized the lyrics as quickly as I had heard them, the political ones, the narrative ones, the love songs. Unlike the first album, which was almost completely given over to the Marcels' songs about ordinary Quebecers, this one featured work that one reviewer said was a cross between a "Julienesque love song to Quebec" and a "manifesto the FLQ would be proud of." Side One was the love song side, and featured two original pieces by Bijou, "Premier Cri" and "Je l'aime, je l'aime, j'le veux." Side Two was the political side, with images of gulags, white negroes, winter and *fleur de lys*.

Depending on how the question of Quebec nationalism fared in the polls over subsequent years, tunes from
either Side Two or Side One got play on Rock Détente and
some French oldies stations. The summer of 1976, however, Side Two was all anyone could talk about. "*As-tu
déjà entendu quelqu'chose de même?*"

And of course, no one had. The group's use of traditional instruments to evoke ancestral music — the songs
sung in farmhouse kitchens, on the porch steps of the
hunting chalet, around a fire on the shore of the lake at
La Tuque — created on *Bleu et blanc* an unaffected purity
any Quebecer, even a new immigrant as young as I, could
feel with his heart. Through the timbre of his voice and
his choice to use dialect, particularly on "Toujours hiver," Marcel Royal told his listeners not just a story but a
story about the story. Marcel didn't just sing about snow
piled higher than the telephone lines along the highway
through Thetford Mines. With every listen over the years,
I came to conclude he was saying this is Quebec and this
is how we talk and sing and live and love.

The language of our lives and the language of our culture and the language of our songs, Beaupré taught me,
are one and the same. *Mon pays c'est l'hiver*, but language
is the hearth. In the heat of 1976, I hadn't developed the
words to grasp this in my head. But in the language of my
heart, I knew. Even though I was born in Massachusetts,
I'd had it drummed in my head I was a Quebecer. Preserv-
ing my language, this was tantamount, and perhaps as
much a reason my father chose to leave the United States
as the reality that there was work back home in Quebec.
Beaupré had insinuated itself into the centre of the language debate of Quebec just by recording an album. They
had, in a manner of singing, become Quebec.

What had come before them, after all? Frenchified rock'n'roll, *c'est tout*: translations of big U.S. hits — Jesus, I can remember "Quelqu'un à aimer," a version of Jefferson Airplane's "Somebody To Love" by Ginette Reno — and Quebec versions of styles made popular elsewhere, *mesdames et messieurs je vous présente les Classels*! or *mesdames et messieurs je vous présente* the Haunted. What wasn't reinvented English or American pop was an import from France — Françoise Hardy, Michel Polnareff, Michel Sardon, Dalida. As Quebec as they were, Claude Léveillée and Claude Dubois were French vocalists, I don't care how admired Dubois is among the Hell's Angels back in Sorel.

Beaupré wasn't a spontaneous generation. Folk-rock was in the air, in the water, for a half-generation already, in the blood of youth around the world — the United States, Mexico, Czechoslovakia, France, Italy — caught up in the war against the War, the war against the Man, the war against Racism. Folk music drove a beater down Highway 61, drew a left and pulled into Greenwich Village. The folk I knew, the plugged-in folk of the 1970s, descended the blue-ridged mountains of the southeastern United States on the back of James Taylor; it drifted in on a prairie wind called Ian Tyson. It fought its way upstream from the Gaspé, barrelled down the 401 to Toronto, rode rail to Vancouver and then thumbed its way back. It spawned Harmonium, Plume Latraverse and Jim et Bertrand, and Pierre Flynn's Octobre also, even if they sounded occasionally like purple King Crimson. And despite Octobre's having named itself after one of the saddest moments of the independence movement, none of them — not a one, neither group nor solo act, especially not a solo act (what kind of metaphor would that have been? We rose and fell, lived and died, spoke and sang in Quebec as a collective) — had bridged the political and the cultural as did Beaupré.

"I had wanted to write simple love songs. And for me, Side One, that's all it was," Bijou argued with me many years after the album had come out. We were in our basement studio, she on one of the keyboards, me on a guitar, reclined on the couch like a sultan. We were working on a song, a love song with a narrative. I had said I thought we should approach the bridge, move from the verse to the final chorus, the way she had with the middle eight in "Je l'aime." She thought not.

"Yes, of course it was," I said. "But nothing lives in a vacuum."

"Speaking of vacuuming ..."

"I didn't."

"I know you didn't."

"No. I mean I didn't say anything about vacuuming."

She pursed her lips. "How is it I have to do all the child care and all the housework?"

"Child care?" I said. "Laurence is almost 16 years old!"

"I still do all the vacuuming, and all the cleaning. I still empty the cat litter."

"I cook."

"You always say that."

"And I shop."

"And you always say that, too."

My turn to smile.

She threw her pencil at me.

"The songs on the first side of *Bleu et blanc* were love songs, but you can't take them out of their political context."

She shook her head. " 'Premier Cri' was about a child's birth. It was —"

"— about the birth of a nation," I said.

Bijou ran a hand through her hair, swept it away from her eyes. It was long now. The year before it was short. She had a face that could handle any length of hair — and eyes that would challenge a husband who didn't love any length of hair.

"You can't separate a song from the times in which it was written, from its writer — or, for most people, even from the performer," I said. "'Have I Told You Lately (That I Love You)' is a Van Morrison prayer to God."

"*Mais pas quand Rod le Mod le chante,*" she said. "Misha, if 'Premier Cri' had been solely a political song, people wouldn't still listen to it. It remains popular, the radio stations play it and listeners ask for it because it is a love song."

"Yes, absolutely, it's a love song ... with political overtones that, if you hear them, makes you appreciate it more. If a song doesn't grab the listener on more than one level, it's a novelty. It's 'This Diamond Ring' or 'The Night Chicago Died.' 'Turn the Page' works because it's more than a song about a guy on the road. Hell, it even kinda worked when René and Natha —"

"You don't want to go there." Bijou wagged a finger at me.

"A song has a persona. To be successful it must have as many round sides and jagged edges as a man or a marriage. If a wine doesn't have a complex body, it's grape juice. That's all I'm saying."

"I doubt that," Bijou said. She put her score sheet on the keyboard, got up and walked toward me. She bent down, placed her right hand on my lap and, with her left, picked up her pencil. Then she rose, turned to me, and planted a lingering kiss on my lips. She tapped the eraser end of the pencil against my temple and said, "This is why I love you." Then she grabbed the crotch of my jeans. "This is why I keep you."

"See how complex a man I am?"

Of course she was right to doubt I would say no more on the subject. For a marriage to last, conversation can never end with "that's all I'm saying."

Bleu et blanc was very much on my mind in 1976. The album was a slow burn, released in the summer of the previous year; the Love Song side got more play early on. But as the new year warmed and everyone talked about the possibility of elections — how would Lévesque force down Bourassa? — the Political Song side of the album, the one that shouted from the top of the emptying corporate towers of Montreal — "We refuse to be defined except by how we define ourselves" — began to get more airplay. No one talked then about referendums. That would have been out of step, out of order. First would come the election, then would come the laws to solidify French culture and language and schools. And then, as surely as one note, one measure, one word follows another, independence would come.

As school's end neared, I looked forward to the Beaupré concert and I had persuaded Norman, Louise and her friend Alexandria that they should come with me on the last night of the big St. Jean party at Beaver Lake. Norman and I, when we weren't with the rest of Les Choristes, spent a lot of time together that spring. It was Norman who got me to stop smoking — it was incompatible with the image, or lung capacity, of an athlete, he'd said, not that either of us was ever very athletic. Still, not noticing the contradiction, it was often Norman and I who were the ones to approach older teens to buy beer for us at the *épicerie*. It was never the same store twice in a row and we tried not to buy at places we frequented on errands for our families. This meant some walking on our part or taking the bus. The night of the Saturday concert for *la fête nationale*, we would be dry, however. The girls didn't like hanging around with us when we drank.

Near the new Pie IX station we took the bus all the way up Mount Royal Avenue. Norman was sweet on Louise, who had grown taller since grade school so that her big tits no longer seemed big but well proportioned. She and I had advanced not much further than the kissing of two summers previous, and we had agreed through words spoken, misspoken and unspoken, in language only teens can figure out, that it was okay to see other people. Still, Norman had felt obliged not to ask Louise to be his date before checking with me. "I swear it's just friends," he'd said. "*Hé, Norman, c'est cool.*" In any case, I kind of had to be cool with it: One, I was with Alexandria, who was new to the school, and two, since our parents reminded us that we were still minors, we were all accompanied by Louise's older sister, Denise, and her boyfriend, Victor.

Sundays in the summer, the Mount Royal and Park Avenue buses always smelled. The scents were of bread and garlic and chicken, salt pork and spicy sausage, the odours emanating from the large wicker baskets the Italian and Greek families — roly-poly father, string-bean mother (or vice-versa), thin, dark-haired and dark-skinned children — carried with them up the mountain for picnics. Saturdays, it was to Jeanne-Mance Park for soccer games, the families spreading their blankets and baskets on the grass while the younger fathers, the ones who weren't so roly-poly and the older sons, the teens and the ones in their 20s, kicked the white-and-black orb like the players back home. The 80 and the 97 were the immigrants' buses, taking them to their family pleasures on the weekends and back to their triplex-apartment homes in Park Ex, and the Italian and Portuguese neighbourhoods ("Littles" each although they loomed large in imagination and identity) along St. Laurent.

When we piled onto the 97, it was jammed already with people headed to the mountain for the concert. Harmonium, Richard Séguin, Octobre, they were all going to be there. Harmonium was the headliner, but I was there for Beaupré. It'd been a year since their second album had come out. Would they sound like they did on their albums? Would they sing anything from the first album or just off *Bleu et blanc*? Would they sing anything new? What would Bijou look like up close? We grabbed our bus transfers and squeezed into the middle. People around us were ready for a warm night, in dresses, short sleeves, jeans and cut-offs. Every other person it seemed had a blue and white flag, the *fleurdelisé*. I saw a few faces I recognized from church and the neighbourhood.

From the back of the bus, I recognized a familiar laugh and taunting voice. Marc sat with a group of kids I'd never seen before and he pointed to a family nearby but not facing him. He pointed, held his nose, and laughed. "*Que ça sent mauvais*," he said. "*Ah, c'est l'ail! C'est l'ail des immigrants.*"

I moved behind Alexandria, so we were both facing front. She was an inch or two shorter than I. She had hair as black as Cleopatra's. She smelled faintly of lavender.

"Marc," I said.

"*J'sais*," Norman said. His jaw was clenched. "What an asshole."

"Who's that?" said Alex, which is what we called her. The teachers called her Alexandria. Her father, an engineer, had worked once in Egypt.

"It's Marc," I said.

"I thought you were friends."

"Sometimes I wonder," I said.

"I should clobber him," Norman said.

Louise looked up at him over her shoulder. Already, there was a look of tenderness in her eyes. I wondered if she knew about his uncle. Louise glanced at me. She would have remembered how I felt about Marc, but then, she would have known, too, that I still hung around with him.

There was an opener, followed by Séguin, and then Octobre. There was a break before Beaupré went on. The air was light. The heat of the early summer day had given way to a coolness, measured not only in temperature but in the hip greetings of friends, in the jazzy-rock and folk-rock harmonics onstage, in the pungent yet sweet penetration of marijuana, in the distant static sound of "Silly Love Songs" on a transistor. The marijuana wasn't as off in the distance as the Paul McCartney, I began to notice. Smoke drifted around us, and through the churchlike canopy of leaves like an unholy incense. Denise's boyfriend Victor took a pack of cigarettes out of his shirt pocket, flipped open the box top and slid out a thin unfiltered cigarette. "Ah, Victor, *j'sais pas*," Denise said, as she looked at her eager charges.

"Denise, it's no big deal. Just a little weed."

He lit the fragile-looking cigarette, held it between his thumb and index finger, brought it to his thin, puckered lips and inhaled deeply. It caused a comet burn at the tip. He closed his lips in a tight smile, swallowed without exhaling the smoke, and passed the cigarette to Denise. As she toked, he released the smoke that had gathered in his lungs, a thin stream that shaped a cloud over the four of us. "That's how you do it," he said.

"Vic," Denise said.

"*C'est mieux qu'ils le fassent devant toé,*" he said. "You know? Lead by example, I always say."

About nine, Beaupré took the stage. They wore the blue denim outfits of *bûcherons* from James Bay. Bijou had added a knitted white tuque. Her blonde hair fell in stellar streams to her waist, and swayed with every move of her body at the keyboard. I saw grace notes alight from Bijou's piano and rise, stringing flight companions from along the staves, musical birds on wires, as they ascended into the midnight above Mount Royal, until I couldn't see or hear them anymore. Sometimes they were soap bubbles, which rose then popped in the branches of the trees beneath the light of the cross.

Marcel Beaupré directed the band from the courtside of Marcel Royal, with whom he traded the lead on vocals and guitar. His propulsive play lifted the band like an elk risen to meet its first snowfall; then at times, it seemed as if he had moved side by side with the melody, allowing it to speed ahead and then running to catch up, a pair of squirrels in a chase around a tree trunk. And though he gave each song a constancy, he added colours just under the melody so when the group launched into "Objet d'art" from the first album, I felt myself as if enveloped within a Riopelle oil. Or when he put his thumb through the electrified palette of "Le Serpent à plumes," from *Bleu et blanc*, I saw the tongues of red and orange in the dragon's wings, tail and fiery mouth. Was I high on *la marijuana*, or was it Beaupré? I would have to say both.

"*Hé, est-ce-qu'on a apporté quelqu'chose à manger*?" I asked.

Victor and Denise giggled. "Someone's got the munchies," she said. Victor lit another cigarette, inverted it and cast the burning end into his mouth. Denise put her mouth on his, over the end of the cigarette, and Victor blew a smoky kiss into it. Alex elbowed me. "*Veux-tu l'essayer*?" Victor offered me the cigarette and I blew smoke into Alex's mouth as it tentatively covered mine. She did the same for me, and then she turned and opened her mouth to Norman. When she removed the joint, I took it before she handed it to Norman. I placed it in my mouth and offered myself to Louise. She placed her mouth on mine, a fit as comfortable as slipping into a pair of jeans, a fit I knew, had known. We stood closely. I could feel her breasts graze my chest. I touched her hand. I could feel the heat of the shrunken comet nearing my lips, wondered if Louise felt it, too.

There was a loud cry from the crowd. Beaupré's Québécois folk-rock, the kitchen harmonies, the down-home lyricism, had won over the crowd. They were leaving the stage. I looked at my watch. Was it over already? In my time-busting, marijuana- and Louise-infused bliss, had I missed the entire show? The crowd kept at it, chanting, clapping, a hundred thousand or more yellow-orange fireflies flickering in the summer night. Then the lights went out and a roar swept through the crowd. They had returned. Marcel Royal stood at the mic. "*Je vous présente Bijou*," he said. We grew quiet. Bijou sat at the piano and sang "Premier Cri" and "Je l'aime, je l'aime, j'le veux." The six of us — Denise, Victor, Alex, me, Louise and Norman — held hands and let her sweep our hearts away.

There were hundreds of thousands of us on the mountain that night in late June, so there were perhaps that many individual responses to the music. Harmonium graciously opened its stage to Beaupré and Octobre for the last song and then invited Gilles Vigneault, who had performed among *"les cinq géants"* on the first night of the festival, to join all of them on stage for a rendition of our new national anthem. When they launched into our national birthday song — party-wrapped, no copyright on the ribbon or bows, for all to share: "Gens du pays" — the music built a bridge between us all and we became one heart, one voice and one conviction. We knew who we were. As we reached the refrain, "*Gens du pays, c'est votre tour, de vous laisser parler d'amour*," I had Alex's hand in one hand and Louise's in the other.

On the way off the mountain, we saw Marc and his new friends again. They were dancing in a circle, a quart of Labatt 50 making the rounds, a transistor playing beach music on the ground in the centre of their party. They were doing that dance where the dancers pretend to swim or hold their nose with one hand, the other arm outstretched above, and bend at the knee as if they were underwater. "*Hé*," I said.

Marc looked up. "Is this how your uncle did it?" he taunted. Marc did the underwater dance, pointed at Norman and laughed. Norman started for him. Victor and

I held him back. Louise touched Norman at the elbow and he softened.

There was no softness in my father's eyes, however, when I turned the knob and pushed open the kitchen door. "Do you have any idea what time it is?"

Whatever mist had clouded my head dissipated. What had been starry-eyed was now clear in the kitchen light. I looked at the wall clock. "Looks like one," I said.

"Where were you?"

I edged by the counter past my father, who stood near the door.

"I was at the concert," I said. "On the mountain. I told you that."

"Don't speak to me that way," he said. He moved closer to me.

"Like what? I was just answering you." I worked my way toward the kitchen table. My room was down the hall on the other side.

My father followed. "You have a tone in your voice I don't appreciate. And what's that smell?"

"What do you mean? What smell?"

We both circled the table now. I heard the creak of my parents' bed. My mother was getting up.

"I smell smoke. Have you been smoking?"

"No," I said. "We were with Louise's sister. Her boyfriend smokes."

"No," he said. "It's on your clothes. C'mere."

He reached for me. His arm swept past mine. His fingertips grazed against the young hair on my forearm. I moved faster. He gave chase. He stopped, turned, tried to get me as I circled. But I turned, too, and went the other way.

"What are you doing?" my mother shouted.

My father stopped. I stopped. "*Va te coucher*," my father commanded. "This doesn't concern you."

"You lay one finger on him," she started.

He turned toward her. "Or what —"

"You —"

I escaped the orbit of the table and ran to my room.

"See what you've done!" he shouted.

He stormed down the hall behind me and stopped at my door. He turned the knob. "Open this door."

"No."

"Open it now, young man, or you are in deep trouble."

I stood with my hands against the door, braced myself with my legs, and matched his attempts to push open the locked door with all I had. In my mind I could feel the door bend, as if it would give in to his will. But I would not. I had done nothing wrong. Again and again and again, a refrain I'd heard all my life. "Get over here, young man," "You've done it now, boy," "I'm not through with you yet."

"That's it. You're grounded. No more concerts. No more guitar. No more records. No more music."

Each "no" pierced the wood of the door.

"And Saturday, you're coming with me."

The pressure against the door eased and as he left I heard his slippers scrape against the floor and the bit of dirt I must have brought in under my shoes.

We were into boxing that summer. Even Marc had to agree that the U.S. boxing team was golden. There was Sugar Ray Leonard and the Spinks brothers, who were anything but sugary. Their theory of the sweet science was an experiment in how much pounding a head can take. Marc and the rest of us Choristes — disbanded in terms of musical ambitions, but stuck with the name — now met regularly in the Truffauts' basement to work out in the gym Marc had rigged. He had dumbbells, which we jerked from the floor or tried to lift on the bench press. In the corner, where Monsieur Truffaut's workbench had once been a kind-of keyboard for Marc's kind-of play, hung a speed bag and a 70-pound punching bag. Marc had two pairs of 16-ounce sparring gloves, made of brown leather. We took turns in mini-rounds of a minute. For me, who could barely jerk 50 pounds, whose sense of the speed bag's rhythm was as embarrassing as my father dancing to "Proud Mary" at a wedding, whose wrists caved in each time I struck the punching dummy, a minute round meant a subsequent hour of aches in my shoulders, upper arms, wrists, chest, legs and head. In short: all of me. Yet such is the power of the peer group that I participated. We all participated.

Some afternoons, after running and stretching and working out with the weights, it was my turn to go up against Richard. Then the winner of that one-minute round would take on the winner between Norman and Jim and that winner would box Marc. I'd never made it to a bout with Marc. It was his gym, his equipment, his opportunity to work out, lift and punch every day. He had the physique for it, the height and the arm length and the hands, which at 14 were already the size of his Everlast gloves. Me, I had the fingers of a guitar player, the eyesight of a reader. I probably would have been more comfortable pretending to be a boxing journalist covering the Leonard fight at the Forum, but that wasn't part of our game. Our ring was the basement where we had sung our hearts out two summers before. The duct-taped tennis ball and paper-towel roll still drooped from the ceiling, but now it was the announcer's microphone — "In this corner ..." — before it was shoved out of the way of the boxers' heads.

At the top of the card, in the last fight of the afternoon — after having stretched, run and worked out with the weights, after having made short work of me, Richard and Norman — Jim went up against Marc. What he lacked in height and arm length, Jim made up for in stamina and speed. He had an expert jab, a quick dart through a parting of Marc's gloves, and was out of reach before Marc could react with a powerful right-handed crossover.

We all benefitted from the workouts, I'm sure. A summer of lifting weights would do that. Even I was able to add 10 pounds to the barbell after a few weeks of repetitions. It helped, too, I suppose, that I spent most of my Saturdays helping, under the direction of my father and my uncles and grandfather, build a chalet outside L'Avenir. Trying to help. Reasonably soon, they discovered I didn't drive nails as much as twist them: Given a wood plane I would bring a board to within an eighth of an inch of its life, and I was better cutting slices of bread and cheese than manning the Skilsaw. We started with a pump, placed midway in the lot between the river and the orange-flagged stakes that marked the perimeter of the chalet. Next, a shed off to the side about six metres from the southeastern corner of the chalet stake. Why the shed first? To store the tools we'd need to build the latrine and the chalet. Why not the latrine first? Do as the bears do, my father said.

"*Arrête de poser des questions.*" He mumbled as he went back to work with his brothers. In a minute I heard them laugh. My father, shirtless, crouched in a deep-knee bend, held one end of a plumb line to make sure the wall of the shed would be level. He looked up at me and frowned. I'm sure he was still angry at me from the night of the concert. His face was red, but it was a sunny day and we'd been out a long time.

I fetched wood, often just one length, maybe two, at a time. I fetched water, two pails at a time, from the pump, for drinking. I made sandwiches. I push-mowed the half-acre of lawn between the chalet and the river. I prized nails from dried-out and weathered planks of wood, the frame of a shack that my grandfather had built there when he was my age. In winter he and his brothers, or later he and his sons, put the shack on the ice of the river, augered out a hole and fished. The rest of the year it sat on a foundation of concrete blocks like a jalopy. Out in the woods by the river, unnamed as far as I knew but probably christened after a saint, a tributary perhaps of the Rivière Saint-François, I clicked on my little transistor and hummed silently as I hammered the nails to free the heads, turned over the boards, yanked out the nails, unbent them, made myself busy for my father, kept out of his way. When someone called, I jumped to. When the last of the beer was drunk and the bottles tossed into the trash barrel, I was ready for my father to drive us the hour back home, to my new 10 o'clock curfew.

As the shed went up, the shack came down. Board by grey board. My stack of planks grew, piled up in the field grass by my side. I took my breaks on the riverside, which I reached by three short, crooked wooden steps from the top of the bank to the stone and sand that served as beachfront. Here, alone, I ate my ham sandwich and chips and drank a bottle of Coke and listened to the radio I had snuck to work in my lunch pail. I played it low so my father wouldn't hear. Down here, it seemed I was hugging the river, which appeared much wider and the current much stronger than from three feet higher. Down here, my mind was free to roam. I could take the planks of the former ice fishing shack and build a raft, I thought. I imagined for myself a Huckleberry existence, adrift with a Mohawk Indian on the raft, which would take us down the unnamed river into the Saint-François, named after the patron of the muskrats and groundhogs, rabbits and field mice my father and uncles disturbed with their building; or perhaps named for the French king who commissioned Cartier, sent him west across the Atlantic up the St. Lawrence River to Montreal, opposite the direction my skinny raft would take me and my Indian Jim: our goal being the rushing *fleuve Saint-Laurent*, what he would call *Kaniatarowanenneh*, the big waterway, and its mighty discharge into the ocean at the Gaspé peninsula. It would be our big Canadian adventure, our big Quebec story, and when we stopped, at Lac Saint-Pierre perhaps, or Île d'Orléans, we would eat fried fish and frogs. We would bathe untroubled, let the water sluice around us and watch it glide over rocks and then dip into basins of white, never the same way twice, changeable like time, but timeless, too.

With the sound of sawing and hammering behind me, I lay on the bank. I saw every long canoe that every devil-fearing beaver-hunter had ever paddled up the St. Lawrence. I saw scores of Indians traversing island to island, shore to shore. I saw Cartier and Champlain and LaSalle. I heard the words of Nelligan, the cries of drowning men, the whoops of Mohawks and cadenced chansons of the *chasseurs* and *coureurs des bois.*

But there was no chance, really, of my building that raft, nor did I have a clue as to how I could build a bridge to what I knew was a village of magical beings or spirits or Indians in the forest across the river. My raft, my bridge, given my lack of hand skills, much to my father's shame, would have to be constructed of materials other than wood, joined or lashed together by materials other than nails and rope. But what did I know, just turned 14, about anything?

At some point that summer of the chalet, alone by that tributary, which I would eventually name Rivière d'histoire, rose the notion — my father be damned — that I was not like him, that perhaps I did not even like him, that what he wanted I did not want and what I wanted I would get. Oh, how I knew this. Perhaps I'd always known, but only by the river did it surface. Songs were my rafts, made of chords and words. A good tune could carry me along better than any daydream. There were songs I heard that drew me into times and places I'd long since forgotten or had never known. The Beatles, Elvis, Chuck Berry — these were historical figures to me, yet one song from any one of them on the radio and their history was mine. Liverpool and Memphis became as familiar to me as east-end Montreal. At the same time, I knew that the songs themselves were not enough. I knew desperately, the way one knows, even at age 14, that one is hopelessly, precariously in love, that it was writing that electrified my blood. Dozens of notebooks filled with proud lines of verse and drivel were proof of that. This is my life. This is my song. I would write it and sing it, perhaps I would share it and sell it and make a life of it. I had this rhyme down.

After the shed and latrine were up, and it looked like progress had been made on the main edifice itself, I asked my father if, when he and my uncles were done, we might use the planks I'd collected to construct a dock for me and my cousins to use. The Rivière d'histoire, upon further investigation, was slow enough to swim in.

That's how my summer holidays passed. Weekends were at the chalet, supposedly working for my father, but we both knew I wasn't really there. I couldn't do the work and my heart was elsewhere. Weekdays were home days, boxing days, song-in-my-heart-that-no-one-but-me-heard days.

Perhaps the greatest surprise among the weightlifting Choristes was the spurt called Norman, who began the summer lanky as a sapling and so thin at the wrist that the gloves slipped off if we didn't add tape. As summer waxed, so did Norman. His mother was sister-in-law by marriage to my aunt, Marie-Madeleine, my mother's sister, which didn't make Norman my cousin but it made him closer than perhaps a regular friend, over at the house often when we were children, in the way that my mother, Mireille, Marie-Madeleine and Diane had known each other from youth. Diane, *chez nous* for iced tea one afternoon, told my mother that her son just couldn't stop eating. Double helpings of poutine, huge plates of spaghetti and meatballs, a loaf of bread slathered with butter, a gallon of milk every other day. Grown in weight, he grew in strength, and as August approached it was more often than not Norman who tested Marc.

The last afternoon we boxed in Marc Truffaut's basement began much the way the first afternoon had. We stretched on the asphalt in front of the weary wooden garage. The paint on the garage door was faded. At some point it had, perhaps only 50 years before, announced Truffaut Ice. And the garage had housed a couple of horses and the ice wagon.

"*Est-ce-que t'es fou, Marc, courir dans la chaleur comme ça?*"

"Let up, Ma, it's not that hot."

"You'll catch mono in heat like this."

"*Ma, laisse-moi faire.*"

She disappeared behind the screen of the kitchen door.

We went out for our jog, not the jog of the long-distance runner, but the short run of the boxer-in-training: wind sprints, running backward, skipping rope and running, shadow-boxing and running. When we came back, we stretched down, lifted a bit. And then Norman made short work of me and Richard and Jim, landing the punches and making the connections of a much more mature fighter. But such was the improvement he'd made in the six weeks since school had let out that he had learned to unite what he could do with his arms and fists with what he thought and saw. He had learned to box with his head.

But I wonder if it was his head that told his fists to pummel Marc that day. No sooner had I rung the bell — actually, we struck a pipe against a piece of metal from Monsieur Truffaut's workbench — than Norman had landed a series of jabs, hooks, uppercuts and a crossover that resounded squarely on the bridge of Marc's nose, and caused his first nosebleed that summer. The rest of us, amateurish pugilists, had had them — I was the worst afflicted — so it really was only fair. I think. Marc didn't appreciate the nose punch. He retaliated with ferocious right hooks to the back and side of Norman's head, forcing him to bend over and cover up with his gloves, then with a left crossover to Norman's exposed face. Norman fell. Richard and Jim rushed to Marc and pulled him off. I went to Norman's side.

"Are you fucking nuts?" I shouted at Marc.

"Me? He's the one who attacked!" Marc said with his back against the cool concrete wall of the basement. Jim and Richard each had a hand on one of Marc's shoulders, pressing him there, more officers of the peace than cornermen. Marc puffed for air.

"You know you're the better boxer," I said. "You didn't have to whale away at him like that."

"He gave me a bloody nose!" Marc said.

I looked at Marc's white granddad undershirt. A maroon splotch spread down toward the sternum, widening in an irregular pattern, willing us to see a shape in it, a roadkill frog perhaps or the psychedelia of album cover art. Marc grabbed a towel and feverishly wiped his face, his nose.

Norman breathed heavily and tried not to cry. He spat tiredly. A tooth fell out and landed in the nose blood.

"—calling me nuts," Marc was saying. "He's the one. The whole family's nutcases. Aunt doesn't speak. Father's outta work on burnout. Whole fucking family of loony tunes. It's no wonder the uncle killed himself. He was loony, too."

I stood up and made for Marc, but Richard blocked my path.

"Leave him," Richard said.

"Stop it! Stop it stop it stop it!" Norman said.

I relaxed my arm, turned to Norman and offered my hand to him instead. "*Viens t'en*," I said.

"*Complètement fou, j'te dis.* That's all I'm saying."

I knew, in 1976, what I hadn't known in 1974. Norman's uncle had, indeed, killed himself, walked along the sidewalk of the Jacques Cartier Bridge and, like a high jumper, vaulted over the rail at the bridge's highest point. I wasn't sure if it was true about that being his 11th attempt. Adults tell stories children find unbelievable until such time as we, as adults, find the truth in them. When we'd found out that his Oncle Lazare had died, I remember my mother asked me after school each day for a week how Norman was that day and reminded me to make sure I played with him in the schoolyard. This hadn't been a problem. It's not an inconvenience to play with a friend who is almost a cousin, and it didn't feel like I was a spy revealing secrets to tell her Norman was quiet because he'd always been quiet.

I led Norman away from Marc's. This time, I vowed, I really had to stay away.

I tried to engage Norman in music, but it wasn't his thing. We saw the girls, we went to the pool. We heard "Gens du pays" many times that summer. The songwriter, Vigneault, even changed the lyrics a bit and encouraged its use as a birthday song, and it was exuberantly sung at the birthday party Louise and Alex and Norman threw for me. When school began, *la rentrée*, so soon after the success of the Games, Montrealers if not all Quebecers, believed Vigneault's words: It *was* our turn. And when Robert Bourassa called an election for November, no one could get the song out of their head: *Gens du pays, c'est à ton tour*. Man! It was coming!

I looked out the car window. From my vantage point on the bridge, I saw the Molson plant, some of the downtown buildings, but Notre Dame Basilica seemed tucked away in Old Montreal. I couldn't see it, but I knew it was there — as when Lévesque and the Parti Québécois won the election, we couldn't see it but we knew a nation was there. When they held Lévesque's burial mass in the Quebec basilica, "Gens du pays" became a funeral song. Who could have known? Did they sing it at Bourassa's funeral? I imagined that, outside Notre Dame the October morning of his funeral mass, the Quebec flag had never flown higher or bluer. I remembered my intention of going to the service, but, like the mercurial former premier himself, I had hesitated. I thought: Yes I should go, I owe it to my memory of him, and then, in the end, I didn't. *Vraiment*: What difference would it make?

That's not all of it, of course. My wife, who had for a good part of 1995, I suspect, harboured doubts about our marriage, had, on the morning of the funeral, allowed me to coax her into nakedness. She had straddled me, led herself and me to orgasm, a frantic and feral search for that which had brought us together and kept us together 15 years — just about half my life at that point.

"*Ma chère, Bijou, c'est à ton tour*," I began. We were on the sheets, the duvet in a tumble at our feet. We were still, and the October light filtered through the curtains of the bedroom window. Lacy shadow patterns cast themselves on our skin, mine as white as the sheets, Bijou still tanned from the awkward couple of weeks in August we'd spent with her parents in Charlevoix.

"Too late for that, Misha," she said.

I didn't have a nickname for her. Can't get much more affectionate than Bijou. I had never asked her parents about that. Once in a while, a phrase would come to me like "she's my jewel" or "you're my jewel." Funny, how I shared her name with so many and yet I'd never come up with one I could use on my own, on our own.

"Perhaps we could—" I started, but she interrupted.

"Misha," she said. She stroked my cheek, rubbed her thumb across my eyelid as she was sliding away from me, slowly, almost imperceptibly.

Despite the work we did on "Embrasse" and the money we'd raised for the Saguenay flood victims with that single, the doubts about who we were and who we should be, seeded the year before, during the referendum campaign, had never left Bijou. She admitted toying with ideas of separation and possibly even divorce, but neither of us, I believe, liked the permanent ring to it. My wishful thinking was that we were fine and that what pained Bijou was her yearning for Laurence.

But how, truly, could it have been anything *but* us? I had been unfaithful. In word and in deed; I had lied and I had cheated. And at the point when it had happened — without a new album for a couple of years and with a woman 11 years younger than Bijou herself — I suppose Bijou had felt vulnerable. Old, maybe; washed up. But that was far from the truth. Hell, she hadn't even produced a greatest hits album yet.

"We aren't meant to—" I continued anyway.

"Misha," she said again. And slid away altogether, sat on the side of the bed. In a motion as smooth as her own skin, she glided into thong underwear and low-heeled shoes, stood and turned to face me. She was 45, but as firm and tight as a woman 15 years younger. And I missed her. God, how I missed her. "Misha. *Ça s'peut aussi qu'on n'était pas prêts pour le mariage.*"

Ready? She'd been 32! I don't know. I rose from the bed and we dressed quietly. I put on jeans and a loose knitted sweater, a buttery beige one that Laurence had bought me one Christmas. I slipped my feet into my shoes and, without being asked, helped Bijou with the zipper at the neck of her sweater, a black, long-sleeved angora that fit her the way I had fit inside her just moments before. She wore a charcoal crêpe pencil skirt.

"Should we tear each other's clothes off and make love again?" I asked.

"Have you heard from your mother?"

"Well, that certainly puts a damper on," I said.

"You're funny," she said. "And I can't. I have a rendez-vous at the studio."

"Can I at least make us lunch?"

"Aren't you going to Notre Dame?"

"Too late for that. I should have left at nine. Let me make lunch. It'll be quick. I'll make an omelette. *Champignons et herbes provençales.*"

She studied my face. I don't know what she saw, but it worked.

In the kitchen, she sat behind me, at the island. I was at the counter, cracking eggs, then at the stove. I dropped the eggs into the skillet of melted butter; they crackled and spit in the heat. "What did he mean to you that you wanted to go to his funeral?" she asked. "He almost split this country apart; I would have thought you found him despicable."

"That's a strong word, Bijou."

"Perhaps I use the wrong word. I thought you did not like him."

"I don't know about like or not like," I said. "He was one of the first memories I have of this province outside of myself and my family."

I brought the skillet to the table and placed half the omelet onto each plate. I sat down and we ate and I told her about the spring of 1971, when one year after his win, Robert Bourassa was celebrating his party's victory in the National Assembly and his ascension to premier. Spring was truly in the air, youthful and vigorous and quick-stepped.

"I remember thinking it was so neat that someone that young could be a premier of a province. He was my parents' age, for crying out loud."

"You don't need to remind me of your mother's age," Bijou said, her lips closed and turning into a smile, the first one since we'd risen from the bed.

"My mother. I don't know where she is. Maybe Toronto or outside Toronto. She wrote that she was going to stop around Georgian Bay or someplace close by. She thanked me for the CD I made her."

"*Et Jeanne?*"

"Same. She says her room is always too cold or too hot." I paused. "She asked about you."

She was silent then, her head bowed over her plate. I'd like to think she was at that moment missing me, us, the way we used to be, but I suspect it might just have been my grandmother. And she said, "Tell me about when you were eight."

"When I was eight?"

"Yes. And I was 18, you precocious boy."

Claude Belle-Ile was my best friend in grade school. I was new to Sabrevois, my family having moved there only the summer before. Moving to southern Quebec was my father's idea. Claude wasn't the brightest kid; he got C's. We formed our friendship in the vestibule outside the office of *le principal* — he with the large padded hands like baseball mitts that left round, red marks on the buttocks.

Claude's family owned one of the last farms on our stretch of road — it was past the village centre about a mile past the railroad tracks. You could hear the highway from the field. They were a good, hard-working family, with about three dozen cows, half as many pigs, 10 or so chickens and one happy rooster. My father used to say of Georges, Claude's father: "*Lui, c'est un bon gars. Un travaillant.*"

Claude used to say of Georges: "*Lui, j'aimerais le tuer.*"

I never believed he would kill his father. He told me often how his father beat him and made him slave in the fields, in the coop, in the sty, in the barn. But my father made me work, too, I said; that's no reason to kill him. "No, really," he said. "Sometimes I'll be working with him, I could be standing next to him, and I'll have this flash in my head to knock him down or kick him. Is that weird?" Why not just run away? I asked. Run away to *les États-Unis*, I said. I told him how, once, when I was riding with my father and mother and sister in the family car on a Sunday, we took a turn off a road in the Townships and ended up on a dirt road, which took us for miles through green fields of corn and potatoes. Suddenly, there was some barbed wire where the fields ended on either side of the road and on the other side of the wire fence were pine trees that towered above us, singularly spiny, but together an impenetrable green fortress. We stopped at the fence. *"Pourquoi arrêtons-nous, papa?"* I asked.

"Because we cannot cross here."

"Traverser où?"

"This is the line that separates Canada from the United States," he said. That we'd crossed the line before, to visit my mother's sister's family, Monique and Gilbert and my cousins Geoffrey, George and Gina, in Holyoke, Massachusetts, did not occur to me then.

I repeated this to my friend. "Claude, you could hide there. In that forest no one would find you."

We were in the barn. I was on the stool Claude's mother used to milk the cows. Claude hung upside down by his legs from a rail about four feet off the ground. He held on with his hands, then pushed forward with his legs so that it looked like he was doing a somersault on the rail. Right side up, he said: *"T'en as des idées, toé."*

I didn't think my idea so foolish.

"OK, then, if you're so smart how do we get to the Townships? Drive the tractor? And if we do get to the Townships, how do we find this road? You have a camera up there in your head — it remembers everything? And what do I do when I get there? Eat mushrooms? Hunt doves with a slingshot? Eh, Boy Scout?"

He persuaded me that running away wasn't such a hot idea. I persuaded him patricide wasn't either.

It was my father later that spring who noticed Georges Belle-Ile had not attended Sunday mass two weeks straight. The last time he'd seen Georges, he had a weak, watery cough. *"Ce n'est pas comme lui."* Indeed, it wasn't

like him. Mr. Belle-Ile insisted the family attend weekly
mass, Claude had told me. Even Claude's older brothers,
Yvon and Laurent, who were 18 and 19, were made to go
to mass with the family. I asked Claude where his father
was.

"*Saint sacrement, Michel, dis rien. Je l'ai tué!*"

"Enh?"

"I told you: He's dying and I did it. It's my fault. I did it!"

"Quit fooling around. What are you talking about,
Claude?"

"*C'est vrai! J'te dis*, it's true!" Claude and his father had
been in the yard, shovelling loam from a large pile and
spreading it across an area Madame Belle-Ile would use
as a garden. They were on the same side of the pile, their
shovels moving in and out of the dirt in tandem for a
while before Claude slowed, unable to keep up with his
father. "*Maudit gaucher, toé.* If you handled your shovel
correctly, right-handed, you'd be better off. Just be careful you don't hit me with that thing, damn left-handed."

No sooner had he said it than it happened. It was like
the story Sister Marie-François told us about the Phar-
aoh calling on himself the last and final plague — the
death of his first-born son — when he cursed out those
holy men Moses and Aaron. Papa said don't do it, and it
happened, Claude said. "I was thinking what would happen if I just ... and now he's dying. It's my fault. He's going
to kill me when he gets better, I know it."

Claude took me to his house. Sickness hung in his
father's bedroom where the worn, drawn shades kept out
the sunlight. Monsieur Belle-Ile's face was pale as an egg
someone would buy in a supermarket and not a healthy-
looking farmer's brown. He sported a gash on his fore-
head, as if the egg had cracked, but it was pink, and that

was a sign of healing, I thought. He woke after we were bedside a minute. He reached up with his hand and weakly tousled my hair. I smiled.

"*Bonjour, Monsieur Belle-Ile. Comment ça va?*"

"*Comme-ci, comme-ça,*" he replied. He was holding Claude's hand.

"You look better today, Papa," Claude said. "You'll be all OK soon." The man nodded, smiled, and fell back asleep. We left the room. I suspected it was not the shovel to the head that caused Monsieur Belle-Ile's illness. I heard my mother herself talking to Madame Belle-Ile about tuberculosis, but Claude would hear none of it.

The man never got better, and soon enough, he died. Madame Belle-Ile kept the farm. She must have figured that it could work — with Yvon and Laurent and young Claude, there was no reason it couldn't.

And it did for a while. Until the rains, which forced the Richelieu to spill its banks, flooding the fields. When the water receded, there was no topsoil left. Madame Belle-Ile sought assistance from the government to close the gap between the farm's earnings and the farm's silo-high debts, and when none was forthcoming, she began writing letters to the premier's office. Friends and other farmers in similar circumstances wrote letters, too.

When enough letters prevented Bourassa from ignoring this small farming village and this farming man's wife, he actually came to town. He inspected the damage one afternoon, called on Claude's family, ate lunch at the table, sat in Monsieur Belle-Ile's place with Claude and his mother, and then gave a speech to the residents that afternoon in the elementary school auditorium.

"I don't remember what he said," I told Bijou. "He put a lot of people to sleep, I know that, a veritable hypnotist."

Bijou was attentive as if it were 15 years before and listening to me still came naturally.

"What happened to Madame Belle-Ile? And your friend, Claude?"

I said Claude was always coming to school tired out. Claude said he had to work to help his mother keep the farm. His chores kept him busy from an hour before the sun rose red in the sky over Mont Orford to two hours after it went down blue and out of breath over Lac des Deux-Montagnes.

"One day, he just didn't show up for school," I said.

"What had happened?"

"Choked to death in front of the barn door," I said. "He'd been eating and for some reason he bolted out to the barn. Madame Belle-Ile called and he turned and tripped."

Bijou reached across the table. I thought she was coming to take my hand, comfort me. But the target was my watch. "Oh, my God," she said. "Is that the right time?" And without waiting for me to confirm that it wasn't — it was slow, actually, by five minutes, she got up from the table and threw on her leather *blouson*. At the door she stopped. She looked at me with such longing in her eyes, I knew it wasn't for me.

"Laurence?"

Had I heard from her? I shook my head.

Laurence.

I looked at the car's radio clock. I'd been on the bridge for an hour.

Chorus

La Ville où j'suis née

Since I began writing songs I have taken notes of dreams and nightmares, what I've seen, smelled or heard, foods I've tasted. If a rhyme popped into my head, out came the notebook. If a line in a book, magazine or newspaper struck me as written well or possessing a vivid, persistent image, out came the notebook. My notebook was my diary: mine to read, to safeguard, to draw from, to add to, a bridge to my past, the story of my life. There is, in the basement, a closet with shelves concaving beneath a career of songwriting notebooks of all varieties, colourful Clairefontaines, notepads stolen from the Hôtel Georges V in Paris and the Albergo in Beirut, news reporter-type flip pads, skinny laundry-list pads from the Canadian Cancer Society. The mundane, the profound, the observable: two over-easy with links, home fries, white toast and coffee, the tattooed fingers of the cook, the chip in the white plate. When I was young, at home, I kept the current notebook hidden in my guitar case, which itself was hidden from my father's sight and ears.

One summer I took my notebook with me on our annual two-week sojourn since I didn't imagine my father would have appreciated a teenage Dylan or Charlebois in the backseat. The squabbles between me and my sister were enough. If I couldn't play my guitar on vacation, to free me from the hum of the miles, the purr of radials over the blacktop, then I could at least write quietly and not bother anyone. Unlike so many Montrealers who headed southeast to the New England coast during the construction holiday to the brine-soaked carpets of

cheap hotels, the milky chowders and greasy fried had-
dock of seafood restaurants and the bracing waters of
Old Orchard, Hampton Beach and Dennisport, *la famille
Laflamme* followed the blue highways of the old U.S.
state system. If the cash flow that particular summer
was tight, we stuck to *la belle province*, in search of
bridges. It didn't matter what type — suspension, cantilever, truss, beam, bascule or drawbridge; over water,
country road or deep, forested glen — we went over it
and if there was a way to stop on it or get underneath it
we did that, too.

My father's knowledge of bridges seemed encyclo-
pedic, from abutment to zig-zag suspension. Yet there
was always more: from a complete history of the Quebec Bridge disaster in 1907 including a biography of the
sickly engineer Theodore Cooper, to a monologue on
strength that almost veered into a philosophical disser-
tation. When in third grade I chose to do a science project on the Golden Gate Bridge, my father beamed and
insisted he help. It took all he had, plus my mother's
intervention and my whining, to keep him from taking
over. While I glued Popsicle sticks, toothpicks, balsawood and kitchen cord, he drilled me on aspects of the
bridge: the number of towers (two); the towers' height, in
feet, above the water (746); the longest cable, again in
feet (7,760); the number of wires in each cable (27,572, a
numerical palindrome, coincidentally); the total, in
miles, of wire used in the cables (80,000). He insisted I
twist pieces of the kitchen cord to strengthen my suspension cables and make them look more authentic. The
pieces of balsawood were scaled one inch for 10 feet of
roadway to represent 60 feet between curbs for six lanes

of traffic and two ten-and-a-half-foot sidewalks. Even at age eight, I knew my decision to work on such a project was an attempt to get closer to my father. And it worked. For about a month, every night after dinner we descended the creaky wood stairs to the cellar with its damp potato odour and worked on an area of his worktable he'd cleared out for me.

It should have panned out, the bridge. I followed my father's instructions as well as I could, given my materials were not exactly those called for in the 1937 final report of the Golden Gate Bridge District Commission and my father wasn't Joseph Strauss. But my bridge, near the San Francisco pier, leaned to the right. The balsawood roadway twisted, and then cracked. "Don't know what you did wrong," he said. Neither did I, but I loved that bridge. I sang Tony Bennett to it every night for a week before the fair. I affixed a balsawood splint to the carriageway, kept it tight in a vise overnight.

The evening of the science show, my father asked me to follow him into the garage. "Here," he said. I thought he was going to give me a souvenir to mark this extraordinary month of bonding (male and glue) or, at the least, congratulate me on the repair. Instead, he handed me a lamp. "Aim it here," he said. And I stood in the garage, his workshop/foundry/Vulcan lair, and lit an out-of-reach corner under the rear bumper of the pickup truck as he repaired the trailer hitch. I watched the clock as the time of the fair neared, and passed. I could see the second hand swing. "Don't move," he said. And I didn't.

I recalled that night in high school English class five or six years later. The assignment was to write a haiku. I wrote "Bridge Haiku":

So much depends on
the Golden Gate Bridge over
San Francisco Bay.

The experience should have turned me off bridges, but still I tried to listen to my father's mini-essays, his recitation of factoids, the trivial pursuit, and still I tried to have my father notice me as something other than a sounding board. I was eight. I was nine. I was 10. I was ... The road that was my attempt to connect with him seemed to stretch forever in both directions of my life. But the road was a rail spur, an onramp to nowhere, the Pont d'Avignon that ends abruptly mid-Rhône. And the bridges to which we were drawn only highlighted our differences. I was the Bridge of Sighs; he was a railway truss. Where he took pleasure in the dead-load, I saw beauty. The Golden Gate, for example, at the correct angle, with the right amount of sun setting behind it, resembles a watch band, as long, slender, elastic and gold as a Rolex. The element of flexibility alone resembles nothing if not life. A bridge contracts, expands, reacts to hot and cold weather. It ages. A bridge is steel and metals derived from the ground and melted and molded and hoisted and riveted and welded. Mohawk hard-hats hang from their peaks. A bridge freezes in winter before the road leading to it. A bridge sings under the passing cars. A bridge separates people, brings them together. You go over a bridge and through the woods to get to grandmother's house. You go over a bridge, pay a toll and never return.

I also chose a bridge as a science project because it was one of the only things I knew anything about. But the older I got, and the clearer it became to my father that I would never learn the manual labours a boy excels at en route to manhood — how to grasp a hammer properly or hold a board straight enough to run it through a table saw or draw a line with a pencil and straightedge — the less time he spent trying to teach me these things. The less time he spent with me at all. There was one feeble attempt, after it was obvious that woodworking and model-building were out, to introduce me to metalwork. Once, when I was about 14, I accompanied my father to a job. I helped him lift his welder, a smallish MIG, onto the pickup truck, then slid into the passenger seat and turned on the radio. "Daddy, don't you walk so fast, my —" He shut it off and began a story that started a thousand years before Jesus was born — apparently that's how long man has known how to bring two metals together. When we got to the garage, I helped him offload the welder and that was the extent of my lesson. The remainder of the time I watched him weld from a careful distance of about 10 feet, seated on a stool, my ankles curled around the legs, my unsupported back aching, my hands in oversized leather gloves to protect them from sparks that landed two feet away, my eyes safe behind the emerald glass shield in my helmet. And after a while my father, I believe, forgot I was there — his teaching voice had trailed away — until I myself nodded off and fell from my perch onto the concrete floor of the garage. I bruised my elbow, hip, and inner thigh where the stool seat pinched me. After the cursing-out, the job didn't seem to take much time. We loaded up the welder and went home.

Perhaps that's why the summer I took along a notebook on another family bridge-hunting expedition my father told my mother it was about time I took the bridges seriously. It was the summer of the chalet and the Olympics, which hadn't yet begun. We followed Route 5, paralleling the Connecticut River from Vermont down to Western Massachusetts where my father and mother met and I was born. The 5 was the route my father took to immigrate in the mid-1950s. It took a good 12 hours to drive from Sabrevois across southern Quebec to meet a cousin in Magog, cross over at the Derby Line and down to Holyoke, a city of brick, multi-storeyed houses, paper mills and warehouses clustered along the Connecticut River. Route 5 passes through a host of small New England towns known to no one but their residents and the county sheriffs — Coventry, West Burke, Folsom, Egypt and Passumpsic — before picking up the Connecticut River south of St. Johnsbury, a name I'd heard for years in family stories, like some kind of French-Canadian Mecca, but which was probably just the first big city these farm immigrants hit on the great migration south, thus remaining burned in their memories like a song. Monroe, Wells River, Woodsville and Newbury; Bradford, Fairlee and East Thetford, which must have had some resonance for the Quebecers who fled the mines of southern Quebec; New Hampshire they avoided, and we avoided; — "some other time" I feared my father would say if only because it meant another summer of endless bridge-gazing. Next, it was White River Junction and, a rare treat, a Howard Johnson, an orange-roofed restaurant where, like my mother, I ordered a club sandwich. It was my first: the burned toast and sweet mayonnaise, the turkey and smoky bacon and the prickly tang of the yellow mustard, the juicy beefsteak tomato. I took out my notebook. I saw my father raise an eyebrow. I took notes on the sandwich. A bite, a taste, a note. The French fries that accompanied the sandwich were thin and gold and greasy hot; they snapped under the pressure of my teeth, yet melted in my mouth. The coleslaw was a cold mix of crunchy cabbage and julienned carrots and sweetly piquant dressing.

After the restaurant, my father booked us into the motel in Quechee, to the west of White River, set up on a mountain with a lake nearby. It was a hot day and the lake beckoned. I carried my sister's and my bags to our room, then we all took off for the day … exploring more bridges. The closest we got to water was from above it.

"I'm glad to see you're taking notes," my father said.

"Uh-hunh," I said.

"Maybe something will stick in there."

The next day, two covered bridges, both in Hartland: the Martin's Mill bridge, built in 1881, on Martinsville Road over Lull's Brook, and the Willard bridge over the wide, rushing fall of the Ottauquechee River. I sat by the brook beneath the Willard and picked up a blade of grass. It was about a quarter-of-an-inch wide at its base, stiff and sandpaper-coarse on one side and tapered to a point. I placed it in a flat space between my thumbs, brought my fingers together in a steeple and blew air through the thumbs.

"Show me," my sister said. If I was 14, that would have placed Marie-Eve at 11 in 1976. She'd always been a pip-squeak of a girl with a narrow face and mousy hair. That spring she'd shot up three inches or so. Now we sat in the back seat of the car at almost equal height. Her voice, though, was still a shrill little whine. That hadn't changed.

She sat down by me and I showed her what I did with the grass. She tried and failed, tried and failed, tried and squeaked.

"Cool," she said.

In the car we blew through our thumbs, the tiny reeds vibrating in an impromptu kazoo concert. But the grass got wet from our zealousness. "My blade's ripped and wet," she said. Then her voice pitched higher: "It won't blow! Papa, I want some more grass. We have to stop I need more grass!"

"I'm not stopping for grass," my father said.

And higher: "*Mais, Papa!*"

"*Tais-toi!*"

The next night, Brattleboro, then the big push into Massachusetts, Greenfield, Deerfield, Whatley, West Hatfield, Northampton, mid-afternoon at the Connecticut River Oxbow, then into Holyoke and some of its neighbourhoods: Smiths Ferry, the Highlands, down into the Flats to a lane parallel to South Summer Street, behind the blue-grey four-storey tenement where I was born and lived until I was five. I had only shadowy memories of this place, of sand in my mouth and someone very much like my mother on the wood porch, *la galerie*, vertical slats, horizontal floors, diagonal stair rails. The porch hadn't changed. Women gossiped to each other in Spanish as they brought in their laundry off the back galleries while below in the dusty backyard their children played marbles and rode tricycles. On the corner, near Sargeant Street, older bronzed children with broad smiles on thin faces horsed around in the spray of an opened fireplug.

"This isn't what I remember," my father said. "Where do all these *Portugais* come from?"

"Puerto Rico," my mother said. "They're Puerto Rican."

"Same thing."

"They were here when we left," she said.

"Not so many before."

We drove out South Summer, where the apartment buildings had rounded façades of yellow brick. The molding of the windows and the doors were brown like the residents inside.

My father pointed to a corner store. "Monsieur Peloquin had his store here," he said. It was a church now, Iglesia de Nueva Esperanza. "What the hell?"

At Cabot Street he turned right, sure of himself despite the changes that were more and more pronounced. "You were baptized here," he said. "L'Église Précieux-Sang."

I remembered none of this. It meant nothing to me. To my father and mother, however, it signified the beginning of their lives together, words spoken and sentiments likely unuttered, bowling alleys and empty parking lots, Mountain Park, Look Park, Mt. Tom picnics and Sunday rides all the way out to, my God, Feeding Hills, then my introduction, or interruption, into their marriage. Here I was being returned to a place of their youth. Mine, too, but not a return like theirs. Mine was empty of memory, devoid of feeling and caring.

Farther down the street, Pat's Supermarket, a liquor store and across the way a pizzeria. We crossed Canal Street. "Your mother worked in that mill up until the time you were born," he said. "National Blank Book." He turned right and got us off the roadway that led up onto yet another bridge. "Everybody out."

The windows of the National Blank Book building were boarded.

We stood in the parking lot across the street.

"The windows were shuttered to keep out the light," my mother observed.

"Really?" I asked.

"Why would they do that?" Marie-Eve said.

"To keep us working," my mother said. I imagined her inside, 10 or 15 years younger, hair up in a scarf, gloves on, moving a lever up and down to punch holes into school notebooks. One hundred, two hundred girls to a floor seven floors eight hours a day. All speaking *joual*. "But the mill is closed now. That's what those plywood boards are for."

"Almost all the mills are closed," my father added.

"So what do people do for work?"

My father shrugged. His shoulders softened as he led us up the sidewalk onto the bridge, a short green steel structure. In block letters near the top of the entrance from Holyoke it read: Willimansett Bridge. He took my mother's hand. The act seemed so uncharacteristic, though, at the same time, it was the most natural thing for him to do, here, on this bridge, over this river. Mid-span, we stopped and turned to face downstream. "This is still the Connecticut River," he said. "Remember we saw it way up at White River?"

There was a change in the tone of his voice. I couldn't place it. "Upstream there to your left is the railroad bridge. See how shallow the river is here. Then a half-mile up is the South Hadley dam. In May, you'll see shad coming up to spawn above the dam. It's the craziest thing to see them trying to make that leap. But they do, strong fish."

He turned and addressed me directly as if only now realizing that I was there. "When you were very young, Michel, I brought you out here on the bridge to fish in the derby."

I couldn't picture it really. I must have been very young, as he said. He drew into himself and was quiet, he and my mom, both looking out over the river. Had they stood here like this before? When he proposed? When she told him she was pregnant with me? When they were contemplating the return to Quebec?

It was late afternoon and the sun appeared directly over the river. I took out my notebook and began to jot some notes on what I'd seen that day: the girls in their bikinis waterskiing from the marina at the Oxbow, and above us at that spot, the lonely white house at the top of Mount Holyoke. I recalled the fire hydrant and the children of the Puerto Ricans my father seemed to think forced them out of their neighbourhood. I remembered the laundry, which were sails, full of wind. I saw the women on the third-storey galleries. I saw us looking at the Spanish ladies, and the back of my father's head in the car as he looked at both sides of the streets he thought he remembered.

"You think it was easier for us?" my father asked.

I felt him behind me for the first time. He had been reading over my shoulder.

"Hunh?"

"We left our families, our friends, the farms where we grew up and busted our asses down here, cursed, spit on, called names. You think it was easier for us?"

"Noël," my mother cautioned.

"*Non, Mireille, il faut qu'il comprenne*," he said. "I thought these were notes on the bridges."

He took the notebook from my hand. He flipped through it. He saw my rhymes, my observations. He saw my taste notes on the club sandwich. He fixed his eyes on me and I returned the gaze, fearfully, yet trying to work through it, trying to move beyond my fear. I imagined pieces of wood where his eyes were. Whoever had once occupied that spot had vacated.

"Please give me my notebook," I said.

He shook his head. "I don't think so."

"Give him the notebook, Noël," my mother said.

"Fine," he said. He tore out my notes and cast them over the side of the bridge.

"No!" I shouted and jumped out for them, stretching my torso out over the rail.

My father grasped my shirt collar in one hand and a belt loop in the other, and pulled me back. The notebook fell to the sidewalk and the remaining pages fluttered in the breeze, then spiralled down down down to the river.

"*Es-tu fou*? What the fuck are you doing? They're only words!"

La Plus Belle
Chose au monde

"**I**s he going to jump or what?" I thought and instantly regretted it. But damn it, I had the right to be angry. I was fastened to the bridge traffic while someone debated whether to commit the most self-indulgent act known to man. I have the power. The power to walk up a highway ramp, climb a support beam, and block traffic on a major metropolitan bridge for hours on end. I am here! I am in charge! No shit.

I wondered if Lazare had felt the power in his Billie Joe McAllister moment. Had Norman felt power? It had taken me a while, but I came to understand why Norman pummeled Marc that day so many years ago. Norman's taking on Marc had less to do with Marc's baiting him all those months and more to do with Norman's own anger with his Uncle Lazare's suicide.

Had Lazare held up traffic, too? It was a week before police in Sorel called Norman's father, Théophile, to come identify the body. What must it be like? On television, half the time the family doesn't even look. Just a quick nod of the head. In the case of a suicide, recognition doesn't happen at the side of the gurney or forensics table. It comes later. It comes after the anger; it comes with the regret; it comes when you ask, "What else could I have done?" and you realize maybe one more phone call would have done it, five more minutes over a tepid mug of milky tea would have been enough. And then the anger seeps back.

The voice on the radio now speculated that perhaps the man on the bridge wasn't a jumper after all but a desperate divorced dad, a member of Fathers 4 Justice, which had held up bridge traffic several times before. Publicity stunts. The most recent one had been five months earlier, in May, the announcer said, when a dad had dressed up as Batman's sidekick, Robin, and climbed one of the Jacques Cartier's middle towers to unfurl a banner demanding parental equality.

"Traffic came to a stop for three hours," the radio reporter said.

Three hours? Shit! I thought. No cellphone, no Black-Berry. I had no way of contacting Laurence. I had built in extra time, but ... And for what? If someone is loony enough to climb a bridge tower in a costume and stop traffic for hours, then maybe they shouldn't be fathers.

The radio had found a clip, a Fathers 4 Justice spokesman they'd interviewed after the last stunt. "Probate courts are biased against fathers," the guy said. "They just cut us out of the equation. Systematically, systemically, that's the way the courts work. One parent has all the rights. Only one parent is allowed to be involved in the child's life after divorce."

Man, was this guy bitter. Ask him the question, I said to the radio. Why do this? Why is disruption of other people's lives the route to go? Then I remembered it was taped in May. This wasn't a live interview. He wasn't going to help me now to get on with this lovely, surprise-filled day I had planned for my wife and her daughter, my daughter. Potential suicide or disgruntled dad — either way, at the end of the day, someone would regret this and someone would be pissed off. Someone might even be dead.

There was never any question, for my part, as to my relationship with Laurence. I met her when she was three years old, came into her life full time a year after that. I was the only father she ever really knew. From the time she was four and I had moved into their home on the Richelieu River, multi-gabled, made of fieldstone with a porch that rambled around three-quarters of the house, I was there to bandage scraped knees, balance her on the two-wheeler, flip the multiplication flash cards, drive her and her friends to the movies, teach her beginning chord progressions. It was idyllic, I suppose, from the perspective of one outside that big old house on the Richelieu. As an old writing teacher said: "If it looks easy, you can bet the author bled to make it so." The porch sagged, the roof leaked, the mortar chipped. When I wasn't writing, I was doing what I never thought I would do, what I swore in my youth I would never do: hammer, nail, saw, plane, and spackle. But Laurence was happy. Bijou was happy. We had made it so.

It shouldn't have been easy to slip into the position of father, given my lack of a proper role model. Neither my father nor the fathers of my friends were the type the nuns and priests taught us we should be. My father leaned toward the Duplessis model who insisted the sky was blue even though we recognized the *grande noirceur*. Marc's father was a browbeaten wuss, made equivalent to his children by his domineering wife. Théophile didn't speak much after his brother Lazare died. Richard's dad was always at work and Jim's dad waffled between extramarital pursuits and familial duty. Let's face it: *L'homme québécois* was not master in his house in the 1950s. He served his wife and he served the church. The wuss, the waffler, the workaholic, the physically abusive or invisible father, they were the products of that era, descendants of a long line of similarly victimized, anxious, severe and out-of-control men. The nuclear family had been nuked. I was so determined not to let that happen in the family Bijou and I created with Laurence. But the odds ...

Bijou never revealed the identity of Laurence's father. She didn't react when, in 1977, it was reported that Bijou, the blonde-tressed member of Beaupré, daughter of René Boisclair, the painter and contemporary of the Automatistes, and Jacynthe Provost, the photographer, was pregnant. It was my first encounter with unsubstantiated, unattributed, gossip-rag rumour disguised as news. *Boîte à chansons*, the group's new album, had just come out, and the media made much of the fact that the publicity photos had done such a good job hiding evidence of the pregnancy. Speculation on the father's identity abounded. Perhaps one of the Marcels, or even Vigneault, *le "gentleman" qui va peupler le pays*, himself. Once, with words I was not able to control, ugly, arrow-headed, zero-sum words, I told Bijou I was sick of her secrets and knew in fact Laurence's father was Pierre Elliott Trudeau. Bijou opened and closed her mouth in astonishment, turned a couple of colours, then laughed. She didn't tell me then and she didn't tell me later. After a while, it didn't matter to me. But she never told Laurence and this sin of omission, this great unsaid, might have been one of the hands that pushed our daughter out the door. It had certainly helped.

The thing about hints is that we only see them as such in retrospect. What led Lazare to jump off the Jacques Cartier? He suffered acute and gorge-deep bouts of depression, he'd lost his job; our parents knew for certain of some things, and they suspected yet others, but only after the fact. His job loss was just a job loss until he jumped. Then it became a clue, an intimation people should have seen but didn't.

There were hints, signals, of Beaupré's demise on *En-fin*, the group's last album, which I raced to buy for $1.99 at Sam's the afternoon of its release. Bijou, for one, wrote and sang lead vocal on every song on *Enfin* except for "Incident sur le Pont Jacques-Cartier," which was written by all five members. The song is the story of a bridge sui-cide. Each verse, delivered by a different member of the group, offers a unique perspective on the situation.

The suicide, it turned out later, was supposed to be read metaphorically as the dissolution of the band. "In-cident sur le Pont Jacques-Cartier" resembles a novel in jazz form, discursive, a prolix tour-de-force, like nothing they'd written before and an echo of the worst of the Chi-cago Transit Authority's first album. It needed an editor. It needed the single Québécois-voiced control of the rest of the album. When *Enfin* was released, the Marcels, Beaupré and Royal, insulted each other in the media. There were reports of antagonism and tension in the re-cording studio, how they fought over artistic control, all the while nipping at Bijou, whose work was trumpeted in the media. There were probably hints, too, during the band's five years together, that bassist Pierre Lapierre felt himself more a Pierrette, but his transformation came as a shock to everyone when it happened in the mid-1980s. "You think if I'd known it was Pierrette's ass I was look-ing at from behind my kit for six years I wouldn't have done something about it?" 'Ti Gus joked later.

Sure enough the band broke up. Marcel Beaupré an-nounced he would stand for Parliament for the Liberal

Party — the Liberal Party! *Le parti de Trudeau, le traître du Québec*! And that was that. The album came out, the band was kaput and the tour cancelled. Marcel Beaupré lost his bid and went into television, writing music for an animated children's program. There had been hints, within and outside the group, Bijou said, in between-the-line readings of interviews with Marcel Beaupré, that suggested he had lost his faith in Quebec independence.

Though how unusual was that, really? So many of the performers who led the cause in the 1960s and '70s, culminating in the victory of the Parti in 1976, had, particularly after the referendum loss in 1980, begun to dissociate themselves or, at the least, not talk it up so much. The poets and lyricists found no words to rhyme with *souveraineté*. Charlebois, *vraiment québécois* but never much of a sovereignist, invested in a beer company. Many of the rest, like Julien and Godin, Rivard and Tremblay, just disappeared into their words and music.

There were no hints that my father would attempt to bar me from attending Collège Jean-de-Brébeuf to study music. He'd made clear his desire I should follow in his footsteps and take up a trade, but to actually keep me from Cégep? It was only afterward that it made sense, that I saw the in-between steps that got us there. At the time I thought he was just a jerk.

It had built for weeks. The college fair was in September. The plan was to go with Louise and Norman and Alex, our foursome having remained together although the actual pairings had changed since the concert on the mountain two years before. It was Louise I was destined to be with; I knew this with some certainty. I saw my life, almost as completely as I sometimes saw songs in my head: wife, career, child, house. Brébeuf was part of the plan, part of the structure I had to lay out, the foundation for the career and the stars — those that would illumin- ate nighttimes on a porch with my wife and the stars like sparks from the tips of my guitar fingers, O! *J'avais des rêves j'te dis* ! — that were to come. I knew it as surely in Grade 11 as I did that day on the river when I was sup- posed to be helping my father build a chalet but instead was having epiphanies.

"You're still playing that thing?" he said. "I thought I told you to get rid of it." He turned to my mother: "What my mother was thinking when she gave him that thing I don't know." It was dinner time. We were around the table in the kitchen, at our regular places. He at the part of the circle closest the fridge. My mother to his left, near the sink and just a step or two from the stove. I was at her left, facing him. My sister to my left closed the circle. The meal was the canned salmon and mashed potato (she called it a casserole) my mother made, a little paprika sprinkled on top, every Friday night even when it wasn't Lent. On the side, canned corn, and some homemade tomato relish, the one thing my mother could make from scratch. The next day was the college fair and I'd had to explain why I wouldn't accompany my father to a job on Saturday.

"I don't want to bore myself in front of a lathe eight hours a day five days a week plus overtime on Saturday," I said. "I won't do it."

Marie-Eve gasped. "Can I ..."

My mother's nod was perceptible to all. Marie-Eve scooted from the table.

He took the fork from his mouth, pointed it at me. "You're getting a trade, boy. If a lathe was good enough for me to start, it is more than good enough for you." The fork went back to his plate and, with a farmer's grip on the handle, he scooped some of his serving onto the tines.

"I'm not doing a lathe. I'm not going to school to learn how to run a drill press, or a band saw, or how to weld. I'm not learning carpentry. I'm not learning plumbing. I'm not going to lay tile or bricks or wallpaper. I'm not —"

He turned over his plate, salmon-potato dish, corn and relish on the side, with such speed and severity that it cracked in half and tore the tablecloth.

"Don't you ever — are you listening to me, young man? — ever talk to me like that," my father said. "You are grounded. No college fair, no going out with your friends. No TV, no records, no radio. *And no guitar*. Get to your room. *J'veux pas t'voir.*"

Now I consider myself lucky. The plate could have been my head, given the usual physical expressions of my father's temper. I placed my fork on the plate, quietly thanked my mother for the meal — probably the first time the words had been heard at the table, but, some-how, that night, it seemed the thing to do — then got up. My sister, peeking through a crack in her door, shut it quickly when she saw me come down the hall. I went into my room, and fell on my bed.

In the stillness, behind my closed eyes, I saw flashes of colours, cherry red bursts and yellow stars against a canvas of greenish-black. The colours pulsed. I could hear a race cadence in my ears, like the thump of a big horse, brown with a pencil-like white blaze, muscular and sweaty, crushing under its muddy hooves anything that dared block its way. I drove the horse on, and barely felt the rise and fall as we rode over him, that little man.

I showed the stallion the crop, but didn't use it, and we sped away, toward a sunset that lit on fire the low-cut field through which we galloped, then into a dark green forest — leaves and dirt, pebbles and pine cones rising up in our wake. Ahead I could see the end of the woods. I thought I heard the screams of the old man — from behind me or ahead, I could not tell — and we pushed on. The noise grew louder as we moved forward and came to what I had hoped would be a glade but was instead a deep scar in the landscape, a blackened, rage of a river out of which popped large snapping fish. We rode the rail of a wooden bridge. The clip-clop of the hooves on the uneven, weather-worn planks echoed in the cavern and bounced against the trees, shouting out both our good-byes and announcing our approach. We rode and rode and then after a distance fell into a more relaxed posting rhythm. I glanced behind to gauge the distance we'd covered, then leaned over and stroked the horse's withers. "Atta boy," I said. I leaned forward further still, wrapped my arms around his neck and fell asleep.

When I awoke I was on my stomach on top of my pillow. I didn't know where I was right away. There were a pencil and sheets of paper strewn around the top of the bed. I rolled and looked at the ceiling light. It seemed to be at a different angle. The stereo components, stacked atop each other next to the turntable, still sat on my bureau, but now I saw at the system from the side, not head on as before. The closet, the bookcase, the radiator, the window, the entire room was the same yet different. I looked under my bed. The guitar was there. Out of my fog, I remembered that at the start of the school year, only one week before, I'd moved my stuff in the room in search of a different perspective. I looked at the paper. The lyrics contained wild images, vibrant colours and plangent sounds. As I read the words, they found parallels with notes in my head. I wrote the music in the lines between the lyrics. My father thought he could stop me by forbidding me to play the guitar.

At school that Monday I told Louise and the gang what had transpired. Louise came by the house after school with an armful of catalogues from the universities and Cégeps represented at the fair. Louise at 17 still preferred yellow to other colours, although, perhaps in a sign of some kind of maturation, her palette had ripened to include whites, blues and reds. This day in early September she clung to summer; her chosen yellow was a straw-coloured blouse, which brought back memories of my grandfather's hay fields, of my first summer with Louise, of lemonade and French kisses. Alone in the house now, I knew what I wanted. I removed her blouse as soon as we were in the bedroom. She unclasped her bra, slipped her arms through. I pushed her back onto the bed, sucked at her breasts as we went down. I heard the bra land on the floor. We played this way, sucking and kissing, for a few minutes before she undid the button of my school pants, unzipped them, and grasped my penis. Our fumbling pretty much ended then. I came in her hand and my underwear.

"Sorry about that," I said.

Louise shrugged. "We'll try it again," she said.

But we didn't. In 10 minutes, my sister would be home from school and 20 minutes after that my mother would arrive. Instead, I played my new song for her. "Right now it's 'The Horse and the Bridge,' but I don't like the title," I said.

She said nothing.

"For now," I added. "Titles aren't easy."

She was silent when I finished, then her lips turned up into a smile and she said she liked it. "It's beautiful," she said. I could sense though that she hadn't gotten it. She'd drummed her fingers and nodded to the beat but the lyrics had floated past.

"You didn't get it," I said.

"No, I liked it, really," she said. "It's beautiful. You're so talented." And she kissed me deeply, reaching under the guitar to stroke me again.

"We can't," I said between kisses. "*Marie-Eve va revenir bientôt.*"

I stashed the guitar under the bed. She picked up her blouse, breasts hanging unconstrained for one delightful moment before she hooked her bra. She got up and left and I hid the catalogues in a drawer where I kept my notebooks. There were so many notebooks already, different shapes and sizes, all bursting with words and notes. I would be damned if my father would keep me from the source of my thoughts and dreams.

And I would be damned if I would end up a grease monkey. What was the point of high school if my future was a garage? Might as well drop out now. Plenty of others had. One guy had even gotten married. In Grade 11, five girls in a class of 200 found themselves in various stages of pregnancy. But in perhaps another legacy of that Quiet Revolution, the school asked none of the girls to leave. The two classmates who delivered babies within the school year were absent less than a week. They slid into their chairs in our college-prep French and picked up *Les Misérables* as if they'd just returned from a bathroom break. They graduated with us, one of them in the top 10 per cent of the class. The babies, of unknown sex and name, height and weight, were given up for adoption through the Catholic community services rather than placed in orphanages. How far we'd come from Duplessis.

Louise and Alex, on the grad committee, were determined to have me play at the end-of-the-year ceremonies. The girls recruited Norman to persuade me.

"I can't play," I said. "My father will be there. He thinks I gave it up."

"You can't be serious," Norman said. "What does he think you do in your room all day and night? Jerk off?"

"Norman!" Louise said. I'd never seen Louise's face colour like that, about as red as the maraschino cherry in the sundae she and I shared. Alex had a single scoop of vanilla. Norman had a root beer float. We were in a Dairy Queen not far from school.

"No, really," he said. "Your dad doesn't know you're still playing the guitar?"

"He doesn't know a lot of things."

"Like where you're going to school in the fall?" Alex said.

"Right again."

"Well, you're gonna have to tell him at some point," Norman said. "He's the one who's gonna pay for your books."

"I turn 18 this summer. When I walk into Jean-de-Brébeuf in September the school is under legal obligation not to divulge a thing to my parents. They can't tell them whether I'm a student there, or if my parents figure that part out, the school can't tell them what classes I'm taking or how I'm doing, what course of study I'm following. Zip."

"And at that point I suppose your parents might find they are under no legal obligation to support you either," Louise said.

"That would be something," Alex said.

"If you go into this with that kind of attitude, you might as well go all the way," Norman said. He brought the long-handled spoon up to his mouth and had some ice cream. "Invite him to the show, and then perform on stage for him. Dedicate the song to him! He wouldn't dare react in front of all those people."

"Where did you ever get ideas like that, Norman Charon?" Alex said. "Don't listen to him, Michel, that's a crazy idea."

"*Non, pas complètement*," Louise said. "He should sing, but he should present it as an explanation to his father, an introduction even, a way of saying, 'Papa, this is me. Accept me as I am'."

I laughed. "Listening to you guys, you'd think I was Protestant and coming out to my parents. '*Papa, accepte-moi comme je suis*'." I put my spoon down. "You can finish this, Louise," I said. "But I'm not singing."

Pushing open the door of the *crèmerie* that afternoon, I knew I really did want to perform. But it would be obscene to introduce the song as a gift to my parents. I didn't dare. The triumvirate tried to budge me throughout May, but I would not be moved. They cajoled and humoured me, they flattered and pampered me. Then they bribed me. The grad committee announced the theme of the event: "La Plus Belle Chose au monde." The song came from Beaupré's last album and the lyrics spoke of the love of a parent for a child. Anyone who'd followed Beaupré's career or even mildly skimmed the scandal sheets knew the story behind the song: Bijou had had her child out of wedlock, had refused to divulge the father's name, and was intent on raising the child — whom she had named Laurence in honour of the river that cradles our island like a cupped hand — on her own. In June 1980, as we were graduating, the group's final studio album, *Enfin*, was two years old. The song, a single from the album, was still receiving decent airplay, particularly on the "rock détente" station.

My parents promised to attend the graduation ceremony. I hinted that I might receive an honour for participating in track and field for three years. So they came, and parked themselves in the middle of the auditorium along with Norman's parents. The class superlatives, chosen by the students — Most Likely To Succeed, Most Well Read, Most Popular, Most Pretty — were held off until the end of the night. Teachers, aware that many students get left out of such popularity contests, insisted that every student get an award, which resulted in some new categories. Louise got Most Likely To Wear Yellow to Her Own Funeral, and Norman got Most Likely To Sleep 'til Noon. By the time we got through a hundred names, I began to worry what humiliation would be heaped on me, doubly so for the presence of my father in the sticky auditorium. It came, of course. It had to. It was the last award of a long night. Best Smile Alex, as head of the graduation committee, announced: "And the student voted Most Musical Talent is Michel Laflamme, who will now perform for us tonight's theme song, 'La Plus Belle Chose au monde'."

I shrank in my chair as a deafening applause arose around me, a drum as insistent as the whop-whop of the ceiling fans. I looked at Alex and the other committee members. I pleaded with my eyes, I shook my head. I couldn't believe she — and probably Louise and Norman with her — had done this. It was more than humiliation. It was death.

Then it struck me: I had no guitar with me. The clapping continued. People had begun a chant: "Mi-chel, Mi-chel." To Alex, I pretended to strum a guitar, then raised my palms up with a shrug. "No can do," I mouthed.

She smiled and shrugged herself, turned off stage to look into the wings, from which Norman brought out a guitar. I was sunk. I stood, walked up to the curtain and sat on a stool someone handed me. I took the guitar and lifted my hand for quiet. It took a moment. I could see almost no one in the audience.

The auditorium quieted and I tuned the guitar, then sang the song. My voice was weak at first. I myself could hardly make it out over my guitar, and the thoughts in my head — I dreaded the car ride home, the violence I was sure awaited me — threatened to crowd out the words to the song I knew so well but so desperately needed to keep before me. I closed my eyes and I looked inside, to where I imagined the sheet of lined paper I had used to write the lyrics when I'd first listened to the song. The sheet was empty. Come to me, come to me, I thought as my lips, teeth and tongue somehow wrapped themselves around the words that came out of my mouth. I listened. Were the words right? Ink appeared on the sheet. Then squiggly marks. Then lines, bold strokes, confident handwriting. It was all there. I could see the verse — what I'd already sung and what was to come, and the chorus and the bridge — all the lyrics.

As the first verse ended and I changed chords to announce the coming chorus, the curtain behind me parted, and I heard the excited touch of a high-hat, the kiss of a trill on the keyboard and the thunderclap of the bass that kicked us into gear. The song was over before I knew it, and the sheets of words and the chord changes and the melody in my ears gave way to the detonation of the ovation. I got off my stool, held the guitar by the neck in my left hand, and smiled broadly. I searched the audience for my friends, my mother and my father. I couldn't see them. The audience continued to applaud. The bassist, keyboardist and drummer came forward and we bowed again and when we stood to full height again, I saw, out of the corner of my eye, a door at the back of the auditorium close.

I let myself in that night. The lights were out. I glided down the hall past my parents' closed bedroom door. I could see light under Marie-Eve's door. When I opened mine, I picked a note up off the floor. "That was beautiful. Thank you for such a great performance. I'm so proud of you." It was from my sister. I opened the door of my room and stepped into the hall. I was about to rap on her door when the light went out.

The Friday of the week I turned 18 I was presented with a bill for room and board. It was nominal: $30 a week or, if I chose to pay monthly, $120. The bill wasn't signed. It was tucked under my plate when I got up for breakfast. I raged for about 15 minutes, skipped breakfast and biked over to Norman's. He was still asleep.

"What the hell?" I said. "You don't get up in the morning?" I twisted the plastic pole to open the blinds.

"You look like you just dragged yourself out, too," he replied. "Just lower that a bit, alright?"

"I been up a full hour." I told Norman about my bill while he got dressed.

"Well, you did say that after 18 you weren't going to let them in on your plans."

Downstairs, Norman pulled open the fridge and grabbed a half-gallon of milk. He unfolded the opening and took a long swig, his Adam's apple bobbing up and down. Quenched, at least for the moment, he asked, "Want some?"

I shook my head.

"I'd go for the monthly payments," he said. "You'll save a month over the course of the year, which would probably be enough for your books for the semester."

"Thanks." I wasn't sure this was helpful.

He grabbed a pear out of the crisper. We went out and sat on the back steps. Norman's aunt, Florence, dressed in a sunflower-print smock over her shirt and slacks and a pair of worn tennis flats, was at work in the garden. She turned when she heard us. "*Hé, les gars*," she said.

The back staircases were made of metal, painted black, or the flat brown of 20-year-old primer, the occasional white, and twisted a couple of times between *les balcons* of the apartments above and below. Norman's family lived on the bottom floor. His aunt, who had never remarried, lived upstairs with Norman's paternal grandparents in an apartment whose number and arrangement of rooms were a replica of the one below, and presumably mirrored those of the apartments next door.

Florence stood and stretched, half a gymnast's back bend, hands on her lower back, then returned to her weeds. The fronts of the houses were alike except for tiny differences here and there — a gable, a floral design in the brick, a round window — which the contractor was obliged, whether by law, esthetic or market forces to build into each house. The difference in the rears was in how the individual owners or occupants divided their space between tool sheds and patios and how many tomatoes they planted. The potholed blacktop lane between these backyards and the ones across the way seemed further from my Rivière d'histoire, the one I hoped to raft into the St. François and out onto the St. Lawrence, than ever before. The lane — broken Molson bottles and bald tires — was no different than that behind my own home — less river than effluence, the runnel in which dreams drown.

"I gotta blow this hot dog stand," I said.

"What? You just got here," Norman said.

"*Restes-tu icitte tout ta vie*?" I said.

Norman shrugged. "What's wrong with it?"

"Everything's wrong with it. All painted by the same guy with the same brush. All this sameness is ... I don't know. I gotta find a job." I rose quickly, picked up my bike, which lay on a path of chipped paving stones that led past the garden to the back gate. "*Bonjour, ma tante Florence*," I said, using Norman's name for her, the only one I'd ever heard.

"*Bonjour, Michel*," she said as she peered up from her crouch. Her hair, short and black, peeked out of her straw sunhat. Her lips seemed drained of colour, her eyes were a pale crystallized green, and the smile they created together seemed to fill only half her face. For a moment, a split-second, no more, I saw myself behind that half-smile. It dawned on me how young she was, no more than 35 probably, and how lonely and grey it must feel to be that young and have your husband kill himself. I rode home with her face on my mind. The tan of her skin and the colours of her hair and broken smile and hat and smock gave themselves over to notes, which became the pump of my legs, the circling of the pedals. The faster I rode, the brighter the colours and the notes became, and the quicker the notes turned themselves into melody and melody into verses and a chorus. When I reached the bridge, the colours darkened, like deep water.

At home, I found the classified section of *Le Journal de Montréal*, folded it up and shoved it in my back pocket along with a pen and some paper, then dug out a handful of dimes and nickels from the bowl on the kitchen counter. There was a note asking me to be home for my birthday dinner. I got my guitar and case out from under my bed, and rode off again. I wrote the lyrics, sketched out the melody for the various parts, made a few calls from payphones, locked in a couple of job interviews, and was home just after 9:30. The birthday cake sat in the centre of the kitchen table. Nine candles. One for every two years. Unlit.

Until she ran away, Laurence had missed none of my birthdays. From the earliest watercolour finger paintings of frogs and cows to later, allowance-financed gifts of CDs and cologne, she signed every card, crayon-drawn, pharmacy-bought or computer-generated, *"Je t'aime, Papa."* When she failed to return to her host family's home in Barcelona a month after she turned 18, the organizers of the study-abroad program and the Barcelona police established a search that scoured the school she'd attended, the entire Barrio Gothico, every nook and cranny of the cathedral and most of Las Ramblas, where every kiosk vendor and street performer was shown a colour photograph of the missing Canadian girl. No mention was made of her famous mother for fear that if she had been taken, the kidnappers might seek ransom. Police searched all the Gaudi buildings, the tapas bars and galleries, boutiques and music shops, plus the known dens of cocaine and heroin users. Posters were affixed to public boards and utility poles in various neighbour-hoods, at the Sagrada Familia and the Palau de la Música. Laurence had talked so excitedly about the performing arts and the culture in town, we wondered now whether it was all for show. Police questioned their informants and spent hours with the host family, the Padillas. Mira-bella Padilla, a year younger than Laurence, denied at first that she knew of Laurence's whereabouts, but even-tually confessed that she was, by now, in Perpignan. She'd left on the bus up the E15 and had no intention, now that she was 18, of returning to the program. Mira-bella also volunteered that Laurence was, in fact, in the company of a man several years older than she, who worked part time at the school as a handyman. He was tall, with the Andalusian chin of Antonio Banderas, and dreamed of being a dancer.

Where she found the guts to take off like that, we, at the time, could not imagine. That was the summer of Wellfleet. We sat around the beach house, forced our-selves out to the water a couple of times. I don't think either of us actually went in. We played no music. I don't remember eating. We went over the same material end-lessly, scratched our personal histories to try to find what — in her, or in us — had forced Laurence away. Something in the belly, for sure. Or, perhaps more accur-ately, something missing.

Still, a cursory look at our lives, our histories, Bijou's and mine, would have given Laurence plenty of models.

Her mother had left Baie Saint-Paul at 16 to enter the National Theatre School in Montreal. Alone in the big city, and with no formal training as a singer, she'd performed in some of the *boîtes à chansons* and busked in *le métro*. Yet this was within the realm of normal in the mid-1960s. It might even have been reserved or tame: She never got out to Haight-Ashbury, never did a cross-country trip à la Festival Express, the Charlebois-Joplin tour of the late '60s. Her first trip to the United States was as part of Beaupré when the group was invited to play the Newport Jazz Festival in '76. When the band broke up, Bijou was 28. Her departure from Quebec to recuperate in the Languedoc was the choice of an adult woman at a career crossroads. Is that where Laurence had gotten it into her head to go to Perpignan? Was it a journey to places she would have remembered from Bijou's stories — meeting Georges Brassens at work on *Émilie Jolie*? Was it a return to places we'd stopped by on our own travels there as a family? Laurence, running away at 18: *Ce n'était pas la même chose.*

For all my huffing and puffing, I had not left home at 18. I found a job — as a security guard in a boarded-up mill in the east end — that gave me plenty of time to read and write. I filled half a dozen notebooks with lyrics, musical notations and chord progressions, all to try at home on my guitar.

Saturday mornings, my father dragooned me into work, loading broken and unused wooden pallets from the back of his workplace into the pickup to take home and burn in the fireplace. Saturday evenings, when my rent was due, I subtracted the four hours I worked with him times the eight dollars per hour I figured it was worth. The first time, he blew a gasket and took off to the *taverne*. Mother, when she came to the door of my bedroom, had a hard time keeping the smile down. "Next time," she said, "give me the bill. The budget is my work."

About this time, *La Presse* had sent its music critic to France to write about the success of Quebec artists there, Plamondon and Dufresne among them. He'd caught Brassens *en direct* at the Olympia and the singer had brought Bijou out from the wings to sing with him and perform a couple of songs solo, new material she had composed in the south while on vacation. Bijou, the critic wrote, was a diamond in the rough in France, our lost jewel. His long article hit the right notes in Quebec. It was a call for her to return home.

The article said she was wintering in the south, in a place she had bought on Rue de la République, a hilltop red-tiled A-frame that overlooked the castle and the crescent beach of Collioure, the heart of the Vermillion Coast. Some time before we married, when I asked Bijou about her time in France, she told me about the house, how she had Picasso and Matisse prints on the walls of the living room. She said her favourite room was the kitchen, for the subdued light there in the late afternoon as the sun began to slip below the mountains. And, later, when we recuperated there on holiday, I understood why her favourite times were just relaxing in the garden, where she kept plants and a table and chair, eating warm baguettes with roasted garlic and brie, reading, watching Laurence nap.

She came home after the spring ice break. In her valise, a notebook of songs and poems, a book of sketches and watercolours, pasted-in postcards and photographs. And when she told Pascal Germain, her manager-agent and sometime pianist, that she was on the lookout for someone with whom to collaborate on some songs, he mentioned it *en passant* to his brother, who taught composition at Brébeuf and fancied himself a songwriter as well.

That brother, as it turned out, was my professor, Robert Germain. I shake my head in disbelief when I think of the coincidence. One professor replies to his brother Pascal, a record manager, that he has a student to whom he's taken a liking, who has a certain raw talent, which, with time, encouragement and a little mentoring, could develop into mature, well-crafted writing. Would Pascal like to see some of his work? And my entire life changed. How different it would have been had I gone to Dawson, for example, or further back, if in Holyoke, Massachusetts, my father had not been laid off from the Mount Tom Box Company. Pascal, the agent-manager, accepted the material, typed, scored and placed in a proper folder, and presented it to Bijou, the rock star returned home.

That is how, in May 1981, toward the end of my first year at Brébeuf, two months from my 19th birthday, I happened to be in a square room with low-to-the-ground deep-gold leather couches, one entire wall comprising a window that looked out to a hall and a warren of recording studios and offices with burgundy-coloured vertical blinds. The light came from a number of lamps of various heights and styles on equally mismatched tables on which were stacks of music magazines, audio tapes, the odd ashtray and glass. On the top of one of the stacks was a legal pad and a pencil, with some papers balled up on the ground nearby. On the end of one couch were a rumpled afghan and a pillow. There were bottles everywhere — beer, wine, vodka, rye — some empty, most with varying amounts of liquid.

Pascal neatly folded the afghan and replaced it on the couch.

"Someone stayed the night?" Robert, his brother and my teacher, asked. "Party too late in the recording studio?"

"Worked too late," Pascal said.

"*Comme j'ai dit*. Party too late."

Pascal and Robert laughed. I joined in, a little late and maybe a little too loud.

I put my guitar case on a couch and slid down to open it. "Do you want me to play a couple of songs for you now?" I had a hard time with the clasps. "I have others — not the ones Professeur Germain showed you, but ones I wrote especially with" — God, I could barely say her name. How was I to talk to her? Was it Madame Bijou? Mademoiselle Bijou? Just Bijou? — "Bijou in mind, but I think you'll like them ..." I could feel my mouth start to run away, to race ahead of my brain.

"I'm sure we will," a voice said, and I heard the door click softly closed. I knew that voice — her speaking voice resembled the timbre of her singing voice and I knew that voice as well as I knew my mother's or my own: pure, lively, clear and rich. It was a voice I had heard all the seasons of my life. I looked up. Bijou had entered the room. I rose to meet her.

She was — and is, after the segue of years into decades — so much more in person than the photographs I had seen of her on album covers and in magazines, and a great deal more than the woman I could see from way back that night on Mount Royal. The blonde hair was as long as I remembered it from the Beaupré years, and she wore a hint of makeup — a bit of mascara to frame her blue eyes and a touch of gloss to accentuate the purse of her lips, the kind applied for a casual business meeting. But Bijou had star power, and when a woman like her walks into a room, heads turn, and eyes and smiles widen. I've seen this happen so many times since that first meeting. The light seems to change and the temperature to rise. That day her jeans were blue, just a tad faded and tight in the right places. Her blouse was thin and black, with long sleeves and a sharply cut collar. When I stood, she came to me first, I'm sure to put me at ease. We met almost eye to eye; she stood a couple of inches shorter than I. We shook hands. Hers was warm. I felt I could breathe again.

After Robert and Pascal made the introductions, there was polite awkwardness while we ordered drinks — water for me, red wine for the men and white for Bijou — and politer awkwardness about the weather while we waited for JoJo, the studio's administrative assistant, to return with our drinks. Bijou asked, "Why don't you play for us?" Pascal pulled a stool out from the darkness of a corner and I went straight into the chorus for "Pourquoi non, moi et toi," following the advice Professeur Germain had given me on the drive over from school.

"Have you decided what you are going to play?" he'd asked. Our drive took us down Côte-Ste-Catherine Road, toward Parc Avenue, under the mountain where I'd attended the holiday concert five years before. It seemed like so much longer than that.

"I thought about 'Pourquoi non, moi et toi' and 'Je m'en veux'," I had said. "After that, I don't know."

"Two's good," he had said. "If she wants more, be prepared. But two's good. You want to go over them now?"

"I'm cool," I'd replied.

Professeur Germain had smiled. "I thought so, too, when Les Grenouilles played our first demo for a producer. There's no underestimating nerves, Michel."

"Thanks for the warning," I'd said, then paused. "With a name like Grenouilles, I would have been nervous, too."

He'd laughed, but then got serious. "Michel, as an unknown in this kind of situation, you have to go in with the best of the best — and I don't mean the best songs out of your portfolio. 'Pourquoi' and 'Je m'en veux' are good songs. They're very good songs. I mean the best hook of the best song. Start with a chorus to let her know you can deliver the goods."

But in the studio that morning Bijou interrupted: "*Attends*, Michel. I know what you're doing."

I stopped. The chord seemed to ricochet in the room.

"It's good advice, Robert," she said, and turned to my teacher. "But Pascal and I have read the song. I found myself humming it this weekend even." To me, she said: "Start from the beginning, *s'il te plait*. I want to feel it whole."

So I gave it to her. I played it as I'd never played it before, yet the way I had imagined playing the song when I was writing it. In appropriating the voice and persona of Bijou, I inhabited her and she me. We wrote "Pourquoi" and "Je m'en veux" together.

The song's title, however, had come from Louise, whom I had stopped seeing shortly after Christmas and who abruptly confronted me at the end of classes one snow-threatened afternoon with the question: "*Pourquoi non, moi et toi?*" We were in the parking lot of Brébeuf. L'Hôpital Ste-Justine loomed behind Louise, her gloved hands in the pockets of her Kanuk anorak. A tear had formed in her right eye, and threatened to freeze on her cheek. In her temple, a thin blue line like an eighth-note pulsed. She had wiped away the tear with the tip of a finger. "Just not right now," I'd said. I'd offered a tissue but no other explanation.

When I got home that afternoon, I went straight to my room, took out my guitar and clawed at the strings until out of all the picking and plucking emerged a minor key that struck me as new and I played it, around and through it, until I had the pitch I sought. This is it, I heard Bijou's voice say. *Pourquoi non, moi et toi, moi et toi, pourquoi non* I repeated, hearing at some point the refrain of "Les Chevaliers de la table ronde," the old French drinking song all schoolchildren learn — *"Goutons, voir, oui oui oui"* – in the same beat as the lyric that was now a mantra in my head/our head. And I imagined the chorus of our song as an updated, sad-ironic version of the previous one, with verses describing a love where one person in a couple had believed it was "the" love: romantic, chivalric, chaste, a passionate love. I wrote the song — two verses, then the chorus, two more verses, the chorus repeated, though changed just slightly, the climax of the bridge connecting all that had come before and transporting it to the anchor of the final chorus, letting the narrator down gently. When I came to perform it for Bijou, whole, as she requested, it felt wholly ours.

She asked me to play "Je m'en veux," which I did, and then she asked for another, and I looked at Robert Germain, my professor, who, with a twist in his smile and an upturning of his hand, indicated the world was mine. So I played a tune not wholly mine at all, a translation of Leon Russell's "A Song for You." I drew out the prologue and introduced some of the themes, wrapped and un-wrapped them like ring boxes, before beginning the lyrics. As in the Russell version I had in my head, I landed the occasional lyric before a beat or chord change, did it enough times that my audience of three, of one, could anticipate when I would do it again and in the verses and one-line refrain — "*on est tout seules et je chant cette chanson pour toi*" — I did what was expected of me. But in keeping with the surprises — especially the movement toward more major keys that I found in the bridge — pitch and beat came together and the "*chanson pour toi*" be-came, like "Pourquoi non, moi et toi," a "song for us." Or so she told me, many years later.

I played "Chanson pour toi" again for her many times over the years, in the living room, on the porch, at the chalet, finger-picking like tiny, fresh kisses. I played it so many times it became as familiar as sex, and like mar-ried sex, we took the most pleasure in the turns, the twists, the variations.

For now, in my audition as a songwriter, it was enough that Bijou reached for a box of tissue. She sniffled a bit, then took a delicate sip from her wineglass. "When Robert first gave these songs to Pascal and me, I had an instant knowledge that these were ... that I would record them. They spoke to me like only a few songs do. And Leon Russell! I can't imagine how you would have known that I love Leon Russell. Ever since theatre school, when my friend Marjorie and I first heard 'Superstar'."

I had a sip of my drink; my guitar remained across my lap.

"I'm glad Pascal and I decided to forgo the demo and invite you in to play today — I wouldn't have heard 'A

Song for You' otherwise, and that was such a smart, beautiful arrangement." She put the glass down and turned to her manager. "Pascal, see what you can do about the translation rights and then we'll buy it from Michel. We've done it a bit backward here, translating first, but that's OK, I'm sure it happens all the time."

Bijou sat up straight, and ran her hands over her lap. "Michel, what I love about your two originals is that, despite being a beginning songwriter, you avoid the rookie mistake of not knowing where you are taking your listener. There's a good tension in the lyrics, and between the lyrics and the tune, while the bridge for 'Je m'en veux' seems to perfectly repair all the heartbreak in the verses." She shook her head and a corner of her lip turned up wryly. "You wrote these as if you understood me, Michel. I don't know how you did it." She stood up. "Frankly, I don't care how you did it." And the wry smile turned into a laugh. She turned to Pascal. "*Puis?*"

"I have a contract ready to sign," he said.

"*Bon. Du champagne pour tous?*" Bijou said.

At that point, on that first day, it wouldn't have been wise to tell Bijou why it seemed I was able to express myself through her. Frankly, it probably would have sounded creepy. A teenage fascination/obsession with a woman 11 years older, sexy and talented beyond imagination — well, maybe it wouldn't have been too creepy after all. What teenager doesn't dream of such things? At first, I just wrote songs. Words, notes, pitch, rhythm, tempo, timbre, metre, key, melody — these were like the tools my father and his brothers and my grandfather used to build the chalet. Often the songs were about my father, about me, about girls. Then, using an exercise in a songwriting book from the public library, I tried to write in another's voice. Bijou's was the only other I could conjure. It came easy. I didn't know why then. Only many years later and after several sessions with Jean-Yves Patenaude, a Montreal psychologist who works with artists, did I begin to see why I expressed myself in this particular artistic form. It was — these are his words now — the product of my having been born in the United States where, although French was my first language, I was discouraged from using it. Then, as a kind of reverse immigrant to Quebec and unsure of which language to use, I was forced to sublimate my self in a life-changing move from the land of my birth, plus having had to yield to my father, but avenging myself by having a relationship — secret at first and public later — with an older woman, a mother substitute. Whew.

Many of my conversations with the well-remunerated Patenaude revolved, of course, around my father. Patenaude believed I was trying to explain myself to him but that I consistently subverted myself because I'd chosen a mode of communication my father didn't use. Perhaps. My father had certainly attempted to dissuade me from playing. He would not have listened to anything I wrote as a successful songwriter any more than he would have when I was a beginning songwriter. What I did meant not a lick to him. So why why why was he so much a part of my thoughts, my creative process? Was I, unsuccessfully connected to the man in my childhood, forever doomed to ford the river between us? Did rejecting him as a teenager mean I was destined to live with that decision for the rest of my life? Patenaude said: "Every artist has only so much material to work with,

Michel, one theme that you will revisit over and over again." At 19, I hadn't thought that far.

The next time I had champagne was about three months after my audition. School was over. I had my security job to go back to full time for the summer. Louise and I had patched up. Our relationship consisted of an hour of foreplay followed by more. We kissed, we touched, we sucked, we saw the occasional movie.

Pascal Germain had called: "Bijou wants to have everyone who was involved in the making of the album out to the house. She made sure you were the first one I called."

The house was off the small Quebec country Highway 133. I knew a part of that road, for our family farm fronted it. The 133 heads up from the Vermont border, veers directly west at Pike River toward St. Sébastien and meanders north along the path of the Richelieu for many miles away from the river's source. In many of the towns it's known as the Chemin des Patriotes. I could imagine no other road where Bijou, late of the patriotic musical ensemble Beaupré, would have chosen to live. I remembered taking the 133 from my grandparents' farm down to Burlington to sightsee with my parents and sister, awed at the change in scenery, the prairie flatness of southern Quebec, the farms of corn and soy broken up occasionally by church spires and that giant soda jockey around Henryville; then the hills of Vermont, which begin very soon after the road departs from Lake Champlain — the very route I once had described to Claude. The 133 north of Sabrevois, however, I hadn't known all that well, until the day of Bijou's party when, mapless and lost, I became all-too familiar with it, driving several times south, then north through Mont St. Hilaire and Otterburn Park, careful not to drive over the Philippe-Brodeur Bridge and end up in Old Beloeil, in search of Bijou's gabled glory by the river.

The party was outdoors on the patio and lawn below the house. A guitar band covered Beatles songs. The oldest in the crowd were parked in foldout plastic chairs in front of the group, nodding their heads. The rest of the partygoers were talking loudly, subtly acknowledging the music by tapping their feet or brushing their fingertips against the sides of their jeans, in threes, fours and fives like little chord groupings. There was a large barrel cut in half lengthwise resting on two sawhorses and filled with charcoal. Chicken wire lay on top as a barbecue grill for chicken breasts, hamburgers, hot dogs and sausages, bread, marinated vegetable-and-lamb kabobs. Around a keg of beer were Marcel Royal; Bijou's manager, Pascal; Nanette Workman and Robert Charlebois, a black gaucho hat flattening his curls. I waved shyly to Pascal. Nearby I spotted Robert Germain with Luc Plamondon and a woman I thought looked like Diane Dufresne, which would have made sense, but she changed hairstyles in those days like a DJ changes discs, so I couldn't tell. There was another woman in the group I took to be my professor's wife. Everywhere there were singers and musicians — of the group's original lineup only Marcel Beaupré himself was absent — and writers and artists, a politician or two, plus spouses, about-to-be spouses, about-to-be-former spouses, mistresses and lovers. In the shade of the wrap-around porch were a couple of tables laid out with potato salads, a crockpot of meatballs and another of pork chili, a macaroni casserole. The dessert table was laden with cakes and brownies, some cheeses, sodas and bottles of mineral water.

Years later, I heard someone recount the story of Bijou's first album party and how much fun it was and who was there in the river sun that day. The raconteur said René Lévesque had been among the guests. But that would have been a false memory, based on someone having perhaps seen Corinne Côté, his wife, who was there, then filling in the memory with the premier, the way we fill in the notes of a well-known song when our hearing is interrupted briefly.

I circled the lawn and the patio three or four times, hands in my pockets, just looking, not knowing who I could talk to, or how; I was a lyric without a melody. I'm sure some people must have thought I was hired help searching for discarded paper plates and I admit, I did clear some away. There were others who might have taken me for someone's child — dragged to his parents' friend's party, doomed to spend the next three or four hours moping — oldest child maybe, since none of the guests were especially old. They were Bijou's friends, after all, and she was only 11 years older than I, contemporaries for sure (except for the ones in the foldout plastic lawn chairs). They were the generation that came of age in the paradigm shift we called the Quiet Revolution, the generation that had taken the political and cultural dictionary of their parents, looked up "now" and seen themselves defined. They were Quebec's "It" generation, as in "This Is It," whereas I, one generation removed, felt like singing Supertramp's "Is It Mine?" — unworthy in the face of such beauty and glory, open and hopeful. Could this really be mine?

"Oui, oui, oui." It was Bijou, walking backward and talking to someone but clearly headed in my direction.

"*Hé, toi.*"

"*Bonjour, Bijou. J'te remercie de m'avoir invité.*"

"Don't be silly. Where else would you be? How's it going?"

"Good. *Ça va?*"

"Yes, of course. I have people I want you to meet."

She took me, a gentle touch of her fingertips at my elbow — I could feel her nails, a light brush against the skin — and I entered the circle with her.

The Beatles cover band stopped soon after and Bijou stepped up to the microphone and into a persona; her personal warmth and magnetism, what drew people to her seemed magnified the instant she smiled, shook the hair back from her face and said "Bonjour". All of us applauded the band as she requested, responded cheerfully and loudly when she asked if we were having a good time and then fell quiet when she stepped back from the mic, bowed her head slightly and seemed to gather her thoughts. "*C'était la raison d'être de Beaupré de chanter des chansons québécoise,*" she began. "These were songs that Beaupré needed to sing — at the point in Quebec history when we were a group — to tell the Quebec story in song in a way that hadn't been done before, to bring unity to the cause of the nation. We could be proud of our history, proud of our story. But in 1981, with the Parti Québécois in power now for four years, *malgré le referendum du mois d'mai dernier*, I don't need to write that song anymore. I can express *la politique* in a different way. We have a solid culture and history that I can use as a foundation. I can be more me, more *québécoise*, now

than when I was, when we were, just 'French-Canadian'."
She sketched little quote marks in the air.

She spoke for all of us, certainly me, I felt, even though
I wasn't quite sure of her destination.

"For many years of my performing life I was part of a
group, a family of people, in which there was a lot of creative energy. It was like in the old days, when there was a
team of people that worked on putting together a song or
an album. There was a lyricist, a composer, a producer,
musicians, and a singer. *Un interprète.* Now, we are a
bunch of 'singer-songwriters.' We all want to be Claude
Gauthier or Jim Corcoran or Michel Rivard. It seemed
natural for me, however, to gravitate toward the creative
team, to search out that buzz, that support, when it
finally came time to create this new album. I wanted it
to be more than just me, even though the album is called
Bijou and the first song on the album is called 'Solo!' This
Bijou was more than me. I want to thank Pascal, Christian, Lyne, Johnny, Mario, Marcel, Pierre and 'Ti Gus, *tout
l'monde* at Studio 9 and Disques MTL."

We cheered them. I wished that my name had somehow been in that list, but who was I kidding? I was lucky
enough to have been invited to the party. After all, what
had I done but write a couple of love songs?

Bijou was still talking: "— time in France reminded
me of what I liked most about our music, and I really
mean *our* music because *our* music, which is so much a
part of our culture, is one of the things that distinguish-
es us from the rest of Canada and the rest of North
America. I don't see myself singing political songs. I don't
see myself singing traditional songs. I cannot imagine
myself singing disco, which is dying like the dodo, thank

God. *Et la musique punk comme les Ramones?* I'm no more a Martha than a Muffin. *Cette année était une année pour réfléchir,* to grow as a singer, and a songwriter, to discover what I like and don't like. *Nous ne sommes pas punk ici.* I came home to do me, whatever form that takes. Perhaps a little garage rock*, ou un peu de blues*, eh, Nanette? So no drum machines, no plastic-sounding piano, no fuzz pedals. I wished to create an album as purely Québécois as I could make it — I don't mean the vinyl — I mean purity, choosing the right instruments, expressing the truth of the music and the integrity of the words. We had this with Beaupré, but I did not want to re-create the Beaupré sound or the Beaupré lyric. If the singer isn't honest, the listener will know."

We had talked about so much of this over beers with Pascal and 'Ti Gus and some of the other musicians during the recording of *Bijou*. Late night bottles of wine and beer in moist taverns, oily cartons of pizza in the studio, regurgitated college philosophy, nationalist politics and picked-at guitar strings — always the conversation would circle back to honesty. Most of the time, I listened. This was all very important, I felt — even if I didn't understand it all. Sometimes it felt like we were walking through a portrait gallery of a museum where generations of artists looked down on us. But never did it seem that what we were taking on was a crushing responsibility. We were being honest with ourselves, and, so, honest with those who would listen to us.

I remembered one night in particular. I'd stopped by after my shift at the plant. The offices were dark, but I knew the door was open and I went upstairs to the recording studio. Even in the dark, I knew where I was, where the gold and platinum albums were hung, where the photos were, the one by Tedd Church of John and Yoko, the ones of Beaupré, of Leclerc, Piaf, La Bolduc. I heard conversation but no music.

"— I'm just saying it was only by giving up the Church that a man was able to regain a sense of dignity in this province."

"But it was pretty short-lived, Gus. We're not masters here. We gave up Catholicism and got statism instead. What kind of mastery is that?"

I crept along the hall quietly. I was still in my uniform, light blue shirt, dark blue tie and pressed and pleated pants, spit-shined shoes.

"Catholicism, statism. Now we have postmodernism."

"Bagism, Shagism ..."

And then whoever was in the studio broke out into a chorus of "Give Peace a Chance."

I pushed open the studio doors. The musicians — Pascal, 'Ti Gus, Marcel Royal, a fiddle player named Octavien and someone I didn't know, who turned out to be Dany Vox — broke out in laughter and saluted me. Bijou, I noticed, wasn't in the room.

"Stop or I'll shoot," I said, and pointed a cocked finger.

'Ti Gus struck a dull bullet-in-the-chest type sound on his tom.

I turned my weaponized finger up and blew the smoke away, then turned my hand toward my face as if to check out the gun.

'Ti Gus struck his tom again.

I weaved and turned, made choking noises. I lowered my hand toward the floor.

Twice more with the tom.

I bent over and grabbed a foot and hopped around on one leg.

Behind me came a squeal of laughter. I straightened and turned. It was Laurence, in her pajamas, blanket wrapped around a stuffed animal in one arm, and holding onto her mother's hand.

"*Michel, j'te présente Laurence.* Laurence, this is Michel, my friend."

"*Enchanté, mademoiselle Laurence,*" I said. And bent low. I offered my hand.

"*Tu es tellement drôle,*" Laurence said. She slapped my hand.

I looked at Bijou, who was smiling, too.

And now here she was again, same smile.

"— wrote two songs and translated another one that are the soul of this album, its artistic and emotional centre, and one of which will be the first single, "Pourquoi non, moi et toi," my newest friend, someone I believe I am very lucky to have met, Michel Laflamme."

Had I just heard what I'd heard? The first single? Why hadn't she told me? I felt myself redden in embarrassment and, at the same time, swell with pride. But who could I tell? My parents didn't know I had sold some music. They didn't even know where I was that afternoon. Nor did Louise or Norman. No one knew. This had been my thing to do. This had been *me*, solo.

"It's heady." Robert Germain had sneaked up later. "Isn't it?"

"I'm not sure what to make of it," I said.

"Wait until the royalty cheques start coming in. You'll know what to make of it."

He was only partially right. When that first cheque did come in, that fall, I at least knew what to do with it. I took the family out to dinner to Magnan's. My father had never been, though we had heard him talk about the restaurant in the heightened language reserved for politicians and popes. I opened the door and he entered the restaurant first, wiping his shoes on the mat and removing his hat, holding it near his heart as his gaze swept the bustle and smoke. The steak didn't disappoint. The waitresses even came out with a special piece of black forest cake for his birthday dessert. It was perfect. The old man savoured every bite; every morsel seemed to grin back. All this is for you, the meal, the waitresses, the restaurant, the family seemed to say. Yet I knew, this was me saying, to him but to myself, this is what I can do without having to do manual labour. The waitress came with the bill and I paid and my father opened his big mouth.

"This is my son and I'm proud of him, young lady. He's paying tonight."

She smiled.

"He's got a big-shot job as a security guard and thinks he can take his papa out to dinner. They must pay pretty good those security jobs, eh, son?"

The waitress actually blushed. She took my cash with an awkward glance as her smile melted.

"You must have saved for a year to pay for this," he continued, unfazed.

"Not at all," I said.

"Half a year then. How much they payin' you? They're not paying you that much." He took the napkin from his lap and made a half-attempt at refolding it. He dropped it where his dessert plate had been.

"Actually I didn't save anything from the guard job." I moved my teaspoon, formed a barrier perpendicular to my father across from me at the table.

He looked at my mother. "You didn't pay for this, did you?"

"*Non, Noël, c'est Michel qui paye. C'est son argent.*"

He turned to Marie-Eve, who sat quietly next to me in the booth. And as he asked her if she had had anything to do with paying for dinner, I said I had another source of income.

"Selling drugs?" he asked. "Or did you steal it with one of your friends?"

I felt the anger rise in me like bile. Did he really think this? Was he so clued out as to who I was? Of course he didn't really know me, but to think I was into such illegal activity made me wonder what he thought of me. Was I such a blank slate to him he could project all his anxieties about the world, all his negativity, onto me? The venom subsided. I would not give him the satisfaction of knowing. I had been so proud. I had hoped to show him the cheque stub, show him the album when we got home, maybe even play it for the family myself on my guitar. It wasn't going to happen now. No way.

"*Noël, c't'assez,*" my mother said. "Michel, tell us where the money comes from."

"He's right," I said. "This money was a real steal. I hardly raised a sweat."

His fist with one finger pointed was near my face before I'd finished speaking. "You mock me."

"No, sir, I do not."

He rose then and my mother and sister followed. They put their coats on in the vestibule; he shoved his hat down on his balding head and out they went into the autumn night. I walked down to the Charlevoix métro and took the green line east.

When I got home my parents' door was closed and the light was out. Marie-Eve was up.

"All I did was write a couple of songs," I said.

"I know," she said. "I read the credits on the album." She came into my room, sat down next to me on the bed and hugged me. "I'm so proud of you, *frérot*."

"Don't tell him, OK? It's not like it's a secret, but if he doesn't want to believe me or believe in me, that's his problem. All I ever wanted from him was approval, maybe some understanding, some connection, but all I've ever gotten was beatings and groundings."

Marie-Eve hugged me a little tighter.

"And a mother who just defends him."

Marie-Eve let her arm down. "She's protecting herself, Michel."

I nodded. Marie-Eve got up. "Good night," she said.

I had said the same to Robert Germain at Bijou's party: "All I did was write a couple of songs."

"And that's all you need to do. And if you're lucky, and work hard, keep your head in the right place, that's all you'll ever need to do. Bijou was right. You have a gift. But I saw it as something else. Literature, poetry, song — they're all about connecting to people, Michel. You can do that; many people are too into themselves to even see there's an 'other' out there to connect to."

I thought I knew what he meant. I just nodded and said "thank you." Someone flagged him and Robert excused himself.

I wasn't alone long.

"Hi. You're Michel. I'm JoJo. We met at the studio."

I didn't remember her. She had spiky black hair and a toothy grin. She was short, too; it took all I could muster not to look down her stretchy black tank top. "Go ahead," she said. "Everyone does."

I must have looked surprised.

"My assets. Go ahead and look." She stood a little closer and let her breasts brush against my arms folded against my chest. "There's a lot more where these come from."

"I'm sure there are, or is." I stepped back. "Since you know who I am—"

"Honey, we all do now."

"Yeah, I guess so. How do you know Bijou?"

"I'm the receptionist at Studio 9."

I apologized. I'd only been there once during the day and it was for my audition. I was nervous. I stepped back again, tried aiming for the keg.

"You want ..."

"Sure do," she said.

I pulled a plastic cup from the stack and placed it at an angle under the tap. I pulled. Just foam.

"Oh, well, must be out," I said.

"Not at all," she said. She took the pump in her hand. She had a multitude of bracelets, gold, silver, thin, thick, along her arm. Her fingernails resembled red spikes. "You have to pump it like this," she said. And she moved it up and down five or six times, her eyes glued to mine. "Here, you try. Muscles like you have, it should be no problem."

I smiled, kind of. "I think it's primed." I tried the tap again. A nice flow of straw-coloured beer came out. I offered JoJo a cup.

She sipped. I poured myself one. I sipped. "That's nice and cold," she said.

"Helps that it's in the shade."

"Yes, it's nice in the shade," she said. "Listen, I've got something better than Molson, if you wanna try."

Better than Molson? What? Had she been to New Brunswick lately and come back with Moosehead?

On the patio, Marcel Royal plucked a mandolin, trying to tune it by ear, and Pierre Lapierre strapped a button accordion around his chest. Octavien searched for a bow, his fiddle in his left hand like a longneck.

JoJo must have sensed my reluctance. "I have a friend who lives half the year in Colombia," she said.

"Really? Must be warm there."

"You want to come inside? I've got a bit with me now. We could do a line, see what happens." She ran one of her spikes along my forearm, traced it down the length of my arm to my hand, which was in my pocket. She opened her hand, took mine in hers. I hadn't missed any lines here, nor any passes. I knew what she was up to. I didn't need to fill in any information on my own. "Or, we could just go inside, see what happens."

I saw Robert Germain make his way up to the makeshift stage. With one hand around my cup of beer and the other in JoJo's, I was limited in how to attract him. I watched him arrive at the patio where Marcel, Pierre and Octavien were running scales and finding common ground. He spoke a moment with Marcel and they shook hands and then there were introductions all around, it seemed from my vantage point in the shade, near the keg, with a buxom woman of five-foot-two offering drugs and perturbing a keg pump. Robert took a pennywhistle out of a small case, wet his lips and blew a few notes as natural as birdsong. "That's my prof," I said, freeing my left hand to point. When I lowered my arm, I switched the beer to the left hand.

She caught the body language. "*T'es tellement sexy, Michel. Peut-être une autre fois.* Thanks for the beer."

She rubbed my thigh with her palm, but in my mind I was already gone. The fiddler stood erect with the neck of his instrument pointed skyward and his bow hovering over the strings, brought it down, sprinted it across a string and pulled it back quickly, then stopped. He brought the bow again to just above the fiddle, let it catch its breath for a quarter of a beat, then launched into a Celtic-flavoured quadrille. I could imagine women curtsey in billowing satiny hourglass-shaped dresses and men in powdered wigs bow and prance.

The quadrille gave way to a gigue, an old Quebec tune with roots, like so many of us, in Brittany. The gigue became a reel and the reel a round, then a Scottish strath-spey, then the *six-huit* jig, the quartet's medley resembling a cross-continental 17th-century tour of western France, the British Isles, followed by a long, water-logged journey across the Atlantic, and the attempts large and small, successful and not, to make a new France in North America. It was all there, in the wood of that fiddle, every song played on the euphonious flight from Old Europe to the New World now remembered. I leaned against a tree trunk, sipped my beer, closed my eyes and let the music partner me away. The bouncy rhythms slowed down to the pace of a lament. This one had words, "*Travailler c'est trop dur.*" I thought of Louis Hébert, behind a plough, a leather harness strapped around his back and chest and connected by sheer brute force to an ox. I could feel myself being watched. I opened my eyes.

"Where did you go?" Bijou asked.

"Magical mystery tour," I said. I told her where the music had taken me.

She seemed pleased. "You're a true musician, aren't you." It wasn't a question.

"Well, it is home," I said.

Dusk fell and the group was now a quintet. 'Ti Gus had gone in the house and come back out with a pair of spoons. He pulled up a creaky, straight-backed chair, sat down and counted out, "two- three- four." The band — I think it would be fair to say that at five they then constituted a band — kicked into gear with the Cajun "Laisse le bon temps rouler."

"I mean—"

"I know what you mean," she said. There was a pause. We both started to speak, but I backed off. "I saw that you met JoJo."

I blushed.

"She's a temptress."

"Mmmm. I was thinking predator," I said.

Bijou made a purring sound. "Watch out. They're everywhere under Mont St. Hilaire."

She lay her hand on my bicep and let it linger there three beats. "The party will break up after dark," she said. "Then I've got to give Laurence her bath and get her to bed. Why don't you make yourself at home? You can hang out in the living room 'til she's asleep. I want to talk about another project."

I'd already been in the house. A black grand commanded attention by the large bay window of the living room. There were a couple of acoustic guitars in their stands by a wall, one a 12, the other a six-string, both made of spruce and rosewood. Against the other wall the components of her stereo system and countless albums sat on shelves built into the brick. There were speakers on top of stands in the four corners and two suspended from the ceiling. Imagining myself in that room, with all that music around me, I said yes.

And after the party's guests trailed off into the darkness, after Laurence was bathed and through the doorway to dreamland, after Bijou and I talked, from opposite ends of a big, red, comfy couch, beer and white wine replaced by water, with *Revolver* following the McGarrigles' *French Record* tailgating *Starmania* on the turntable, the conversation dipping and passing, dipping and passing like a canoe paddle over the river flowing between us, I got up. Had I, perhaps, not been 19 (a boy, in college, living at home) and she 30 (a woman, with a career and a child) perhaps perhaps perhaps I would have known how to take her. Instead, I stood with my hands in the pockets of my jeans, the soundtrack of the day fading, my head buzzing, and looked at Bijou on the couch. She sat at an angle; she'd brought her left leg up and folded it under her. Her left arm was stretched over the back of the couch, and from where I stood I could glimpse a bit of her breast where a button had come undone. I imagined us seated at an old oak farmhouse table with the screen door open to the backyard and the sound of crickets announcing they'd begun guard duty outside and more than 30 years of love enveloping us like the light of a candle. Bijou pulled her leg out from under her, slipped her bare feet onto the hardwood floor. When she moved, citrus perfumed the air, and when she was still, I saw myself running my thumb over the flesh of her lips and the rise in her cheeks. I saw the future I could have looking into her eyes forever and ever and ever. She stood. A wisp of her pulled-up hair had fallen and I reached out to replace it. Years later, she told me that whenever she felt she needed to be close to me, whether I was away or perhaps after we had fought, that she would return to that single gesture of grace.

She took my hand and held it.

"What did you see just now, Misha?"

"I can't name it, but I know it's real."

I would like to think she wanted the same that night. I suspect that what she needed then was the brown-eyed handsome man standing before her. "*Je te désire*," she said. And that was all I needed to hear.

Ah, but I couldn't give her what she wanted. She tried, I tried. Nerves and beer had gotten the best of me, I suppose. Instead, I caressed her with my fingers, my lips, my tongue. In the morning, under the mantle of dawn in her bedroom upstairs, Bijou reached over and, satisfied that she'd found what she was sought, climbed on top of me, glided herself over me and found her place, our place.

Verse Four
Musique et paroles

Bijou had led a charmed life. I told her this often enough over the course of our marriage. And of course she argued that she hadn't. No one ever admits they'd had it easy. One of Bijou's gripes was the inequality she'd felt as a woman in Beaupré. But the argument, to me at least, held as much water as George Harrison's complaints about being overshadowed. "You were in one of the most successful groups in Quebec history! On the frontline of the discussion of our political future! Look at all the songs you wrote! The last album is almost entirely yours!"

This charmed life found expression elsewhere as well. Like death. Until age 40, Bijou had not had a death in her family or among close friends. Three grandparents had died before she turned two, so she had no recollection of them; the fourth, Bijou's maternal grandmother, was considerably younger than her husband and still played Bingo and took walks around the block. Aunts, uncles, cousins, all still alive. Friends, still alive. Teachers, the ones she cared about, still alive. It made for a lot of Christmas cards and comps when she played the Spectrum.

But the year Bijou turned 40, Dany Vox died of cancer. Dany was Daniel when his parents named him and he was Daniel Vaudreuil until he decided he would be a singer. Jesus, did Dany have a voice, not one of those European bel canto voices or those all-vibrato Parisian-trained voices like Dubois', but one hewn from Quebec maple, no knots, subtle grain. When Dany sang, he tapped into the elemental. One April a couple of years before he died — it was, in fact, 1988, because Bijou, Laurence and I had just returned from Paris where Bijou had done an extended stay at the Théâtre de Paris to record *Mes racines*, Dany gave an acoustic concert at the Olympia in the east end. One thousand fans, and not one wouldn't have bled for him that night. That voice that night, singing "La Belle Mort" and "Memoirs de printemps" — that's how I wished to remember him. After the Olympia show, we'd sat on the edge of the stage while the roadies broke down the set around us. Bijou was there; my sister, Marie-Eve; Serge, Dany's brother whom we met that night; and Serge's boyfriend, Louis-Philippe, a Bombardier engineer whom we called LP.

"I don't know how you all do it," my sister said. "Songwriters say so much with so few words."

"Economy," Dany said.

"To the economy," I said and I raised my bottle. The chorus of clinking echoed in the near-empty hall. "You never said that to me before."

"I'm saying it now," Marie-Eve said.

"Thanks."

I reached over and squeezed my sister's shoulder. She rubbed my leg and gave it a pat.

"So how *do* you do it?" Serge said. "You've had some success, writing for Bijou. I heard you even—"

"No, no, don't say it!" Bijou said, put her fingers in her ears and shook her head.

"Céline."

"You said it!"

"The trick is being economical but expansive at the same time," I said, feeling expansive myself. "Like a watch band. You ever notice a watch band? You know the old ones that you could twist and turn and tug at and they would always go back into shape? A song has to be built like that. Verse, chorus, bridge, all in three chords and what ... a hundred, hundred-fifty words?"

"What's a bridge?" Serge asked.

Dany shrugged. "Damned if I know," he said, a concert's worth of evidence to the contrary.

"I've never been able to write a good one," I said.

"That's not true," Bijou said. She sat on stage on the other side of Dany, hand on his lap.

"But what is it?"

"The bridge is the link," Bijou started.

"The bond," I said.

Dany laughed. "The tie," he said.

"The connection," my sister piped in.

And around we went, like musical chairs.

"From here to there."

"From A to Z."

"From one to three."

"From the exposition of the verses and chorus to the denouement and the final rendering of the chorus," I pronounced.

"*T'es fou*!" Dany said. "No wonder you've never been able to write one!"

He reached behind him and lifted the top off the cooler. He took out a couple of Boréales.

"Yeah yeah yeah, but I didn't say I couldn't write one," I said. "I said 'a good one'. I mean, give me a good bridge and you've got a great pop song."

"OK, name one," Serge said.

"Bijou's 'Je l'aime'."

"*Tais-toi*," she said.

"No, really," I said. "The bridge in that song is a wedding vow. You know any more powerful words than those?"

"Not on the charts, I don't," Dany said.

The others looked on blankly. "OK, then," I said. "Two others: Francis Cabrel in 'La Fille qui m'accompagne' and Led Zeppelin's 'Whole Lotta Love'."

"No way. Sing it."

"What?! Not in a million years," Marie-Eve said quickly.

"Thanks, Sis."

"Then what's one you can sing?" LP said.

"The Police. 'Every Breath You Take'," I said.

"What's the bridge there? It's just numbness beginning to end," LP said and he made noises like Sting's baseline.

"It's about stalking," Bijou said.

"Yeah, until you're in the bridge," I said. "Then you find the emotional bond. Why he can't let go." I sang. I stopped. I polished off my beer.

"I have room for another backup singer," Dany said. He handed me a cold Rousse. "Oh, did I say backup? I meant you can sing outside in the pickup."

Rising through the dying laughter came a soft, delicate vocal, one I hadn't heard in over a decade, one that even all those years ago I hadn't paid much attention to, so little heed really that had she not been right beside me I wouldn't have known the *chanteuse* was my sister:

Is there someone you know
You're loving them so
But taking them all for granted.
You may lose them one day,
Someone takes them away,
And they don't hear the words you long to say.

We were quiet. I don't know where the others went, where the song took them, over which span of memory this particular musical moment drove them. I recognized it immediately. The change in pace and tone from the rest of the song sneaks up on you like a tear near the end of a movie, a tear of recognition. You're 13 years old, singing along with the song, about the sadness of love (found and lost), and then you remember reading in some teen magazine that David Gates had written "Everything I Own" for his father. And it doesn't make it any easier to sing the song when your own relationship with your father is nothing like what you've sung.

"Now that's economy," Dany said.

We drank to that. I caught a glimpse of my sister at my side. She smiled shyly. I leaned my bottle toward hers and she tipped hers toward mine and the tops made a quiet little chink.

This memory put me in no mind to sit through anything so depressing as a clumsy funeral, with weeping ex-wives — we all had difficulty tracking Dany's multiple relationships — and the empty homily of a pastor who didn't know the deceased and who had taken inaccurate notes from the survivors on the highlights of the dearly beloved's life. In Dany's case, highlights would have included his show-stopping solo performance at the Félix awards four years before. But then again, what is a highlight of a life?

I remembered the night at the Olympia as a highlight, but Dany probably wouldn't have seen it the same way. Dany might have believed the highlight of his life was a performance at his high school graduation, or the birth of his brother Serge, or perhaps an even quieter moment.

Perhaps he was happy having successfully inverted a chord to emphasize a minor component, or been smitten with a rewritten internal rhyme.

Still, I went to the funeral, to be with Bijou.

Most of the Quebec music industry had turned up. The premier sent a sub-minister who had an arts and culture portfolio. Those at the funeral mass, in Notre-Dame-de-la-Sainte-Rosaire, whose twin limestone and oxidized copper spires resembled a double guitar, huddled outside on the sidewalk in the autumnal chill. For some of them, it was as if having stayed away from the Church — rejected it even — they were suddenly shy about this temporary embrace. Or perhaps knew that for all the dismissals of their parents' and grandparents' religion, they, too, would one day have the Prayer of the Dead said over them and holy water sprinkled on their casket.

The Villeray bus stopped at the corner. A taxi waited patiently behind. When the bus moved on, the taxi turned the corner on to St. Hubert Street. There was a sudden intake of air when 'Ti Gus got out and hobbled toward the steps. The man, so much bigger than life for so much of his life — a life lived as loudly as his floor tom — had thinned to the size of a drum stick. His voice had the attenuated timbre of a china boy cymbal. "But you're too young for that," I said when I helped him up the steps and into the church. "Prostate cancer's a disease of old men."

"Don't feel so young anymore," he said. "Fifty this year."

"Fifty?!"

"Shhh," he said. He moved his hand with an extended finger to his lips. "No one in the band knows. They all thought I was their age!"

We had reached a pew and he indicated this is where he wished to sit. It was halfway up, too far back for someone as important as he.

"I'm their Charlie Watts," he said as he sat down. He looked impish, rejuvenated by his joke.

The paparazzi swarmed the funeral like shad flies in LaSalle. The rare sight of the estranged members of Beaupré together at the service — even Pierrette, who was by then owner of a homeopathic office in Notre-Dame-de-Grâce — led to gossip the group would reunite. They posed together for a photograph. Gus's answer had post-Lennon intonations: "Not likely, is it?" he said when pressed.

After the funeral, we took the road over the mountain, past the lookout and down the hill and continued straight along Mount Royal Avenue, past Parc Avenue and the late autumn soccer players in Jeanne-Mance Park. I stole a quick glance down l'Esplanade wondering if Louise's sister, Denise, whose barging in on us had brought me to Beaupré, still lived there. We drove to St. Denis, then south to Ontario. We took over Le Cheval Blanc *taverne*. We ordered pitchers of buckwheat ale and served ourselves from the catered platters of old cheddars and tangy blue-veined cheeses, baguettes, then bowls of onion soup and large crusty-bread sandwiches of Quebec ham and cheese and chicken and tarragon. I surveyed the dozen tables, the stools at the bar, all of them filled with Dany's friends, some of whom I knew, and family, whom Bijou remembered. There I was among the best and brightest and, almost 10 years into my relationship with Bijou, still unsure I deserved it. Perhaps I was the one who had led a charmed life.

"It changes the way you look at things, doesn't it?" Bijou said at our round table in a corner of the old *taverne*.

"What? Death?"

"That's why we're here."

"Why we're here in this bar or why we're here on Earth?" I asked. I took a sip of beer and eyed her over the rim of the pint glass. She looked ready to spill her beer on my lap. She was serious and I'd made light of it. I lowered my glass and thought up a quick response.

"That's not a joke answer," I said. "Yes, we're remembering Dany; but yes, we are here, on Earth, to live and to reproduce and then to die. Dust to dust. Life is the bridge between two states of non-existence."

"God, that's cold," she said. "Did your father teach you that, or your mother?"

"Sorry."

She didn't answer right away. She sat back against the chair, her arms stretched out to the table in front, fingering the bottom of the glass. "Why do you like beer?" she said. "It's so bitter."

I took another sip. It had warmed some in the glass, and the bitterness of the hop flower had mellowed. "I kind of like the bitterness. I like the mix of tastes, the bitter and the sweet, like you and me."

Bijou laughed. "I never know what you're going to say next." She shook her head. "But you didn't answer my question. I said death changes the way you look at things. And I'm asking because I've never known anyone who died. You're no stranger to this. Your grandparents, your friend Claude, your friend's uncle who killed himself. I'd never even been to a funeral until today, while you, even when you write me a love song it has death written all over it."

"You forget I was an altar boy," I said. "You see a lot of funerals that way." My eyes scanned the tavern. Distracted from the conversation, desiring another pitcher. "Today's was a good funeral. The mass didn't go on too long, the priest seemed to know a little about Dany. There was great music, appropriate music. There's nothing like Mozart's *Requiem* to remind us what a tragedy life is."

I took a sip of beer. I saw the waitress and flagged her down. "This wake has been great — good food, good micro. We sent him off in fine style. We couldn't have done better in New Orleans."

I was talking but not paying attention to what I was saying; I was working my mind around to what she'd said about the funereal quality of my love songs. I had never thought about them that way. I had always believed what I did was what a songwriter is supposed to do, which is to find the appropriate lyrics and music to give voice to what he or she felt or thought. And it couldn't be one and not the other, any more than a funeral mass can exist without incense or organ music. Musical context is what gives the lyrics their emotional kick. But Bijou would say this was all rather cerebral. She seemed not to be talking about my songwriting, she was searching out, what? My underlying morbidity?

I like a good funeral, even the smell. In the church that morning, a light trail of incense, sweet and herbal like the smoke in a shisha café in Beirut, wafted over the congregants as the organ vibrated into action. I closed my eyes, as I had when I was an altar boy, and forced out all thought except what colours and smells I could hear the organist play and what sounds I could smell in the incense. The organ, as misunderstood as the accordion or the bagpipe by some people, is a powerhouse instrument, operating at different frequencies simultaneously, combining the slowest, deepest, most earth-bound and sinful frequencies, with overtones that bounce with heavenly delight; so light, so incandescent, they are barely perceptible. With the press of a single concluding chord, the organist sent a blast of air through the pipes, and a final spectrum of light, like a disappointed rainbow, emptied my mind and filled my heart. I'd opened my eyes and watched the incense rise and disappear in the blue-grey, high-vaulted ceilings of Notre-Dame church. Bijou had known Dany longer and better, but I joined her in her tears. The organ's last note faded and died, and the church was silent but for the sound of a ribbon rippling in the breeze of a fan positioned by a blue-lit statue of the Virgin in a grotto of plastic roses. The ribbon's flutter reminded me of running water. I closed my eyes and imagined returning to the womb, sinless.

My grandmother told me once of a funeral she'd attended in the church near her residence. Constance, a girl who had Rhett's syndrome. A white coffin, about a foot shorter than most, was carried in by six high school-age boys. It was followed by her parents, an older brother and sister, and three children in wheelchairs, Rhett's victims as well. Since Jeanne had moved into the St. Charles Street seniors' building, she had begun attending funerals. One, two a week. Every week or so she would tell me about them. There was always a story to tell. There was Lowell, who was 22, about to graduate in philosophy from Université du Québec à Trois-Rivières, when he died of AIDS. He was a regular communicant of my grand-mother's church, which I found rather tolerant and liber-al-thinking for Catholics. Some of his poetry was read at the service, and the funeral program used his original artwork on the cover. Or Thérèse, who was Jeanne's down-the-hall neighbour for several years. She suffered from Alzheimer's as far as we could make out because, although she could regale Jeanne with amazing detail about the dress she wore to her first communion, she could not remember her granddaughters' names. It was sad, but a relief nonetheless for her husband, Gaétan, when her brain, ultimately, forgot how to order her lungs to breathe.

How could I explain to Bijou, my wife, this older woman, who had known so many of life's ups, yet, mir-aculously, so few of its downs that, to me, a U.S.-born, part-time Quebec farm boy, death seemed so much a part of life? And was I, 10 years younger than she, really in a position to say these things? Death is life's dance partner. Take a hold of her right hand with your left (you're leading), grab hold of her waist with your right, bring her in tight so that your hip bones grate and your right thigh rubs her pubic bone. Stare into her eyes and surprise her with a well-planted smack on the lips.

"OK," I finally admitted, "my love songs have an under-current."

Several years later — I was 30 when Dany Vox died — after attending a few more funerals, my answer would have been somewhat more nuanced. I don't know that the implicit philosophy would have changed much, but I would probably have added a part about the inconsisten-cies in my own life. How acceptance of death means also accepting preparation for death, means reconciling with the living (if you're the one dying) or the dying (if your dance partner has decided she's leading). But my father hadn't died yet, and this particular philosophical wisdom was not yet mine to possess. And my grandmother, Jeanne, still among us, hadn't yet moved into La Résidence St-Charles, or as she called it, *Les Sépultures*.

When Jeanne did land there, she was upset with my mother for putting her in the home. "It's like the catacombs, a sepulchre," she said.

"Mother came back and told us you'd said that," I told my grandmother. "She was sick for a week."

"Water under the bridge now," Jeanne said.

The old-age residence where my mother had placed my grandmother was not so much a mausoleum as a college dorm. Or at least a dormitory as I imagined it, since I'd managed to avoid that particular rite of passage. The ground floor was an open space, with orange couches and olive-shaded stuffed chairs, end tables, coffee tables and spindly leafed spider plants, plus the glassed-in office of the administrators. The air smelled of disinfectant and cloves. Jeanne's room was on the fifth floor. Anything higher, like the pensioners' penthouse, would have put all of us in the poor house. Each floor from the first to the fifth had six bedrooms and two common bathrooms with security-handled bathtubs and showers, wings off a shared living-room space with a television, couches and chairs. It was here I looked in on my father's mother once a month. Sometimes Bijou accompanied me to chat, perhaps to have lunch in the cafeteria, which took up the entire *sous-sol*, perhaps to go out for a hamburger steak, mashed potatoes *et petits pois* at the corner café.

Visits went like this, every one: The receptionist on the ground floor rang my grandmother, *"Madame La-flamme, votre petit-fils est ici."* And I went up and there was a millisecond's pause — a time that lengthened like a shadow as the years slid by — when she didn't recognize me and then she said, "I was very upset with your mother, you know. Putting me in here," then repeat the line about the mausoleum and the water under the bridge. I never thought it was Alzheimer's or forgetfulness that caused her to repeat this sentiment. I thought the water was still passing under that bridge. She continued to feel the ignobility of being deposited there, the humbling descent — first the lease of the farm in Sabrevois to some neighbours who could harvest the hay, maintain the machinery, care for the cows and horses and chickens; then the sale of these cows, horses and chickens and the farm machinery; then the sale of the farm and the house, the move to an apartment in Montreal; then the residence — like a trickling away of life, water dripping in a very old cave.

"There's so much death here," she said, "it comes up when I burp."

"Cream of broccoli is never as good as it is the second time around," I said.

Jeanne laughed and burped at the same time. It must have hurt.

It wasn't Jeanne's mental state that had forced my mother to find her a room in the residence. She had plans. Soon after the placement, which was maybe within six months of my father's death, my mother bought a Winnebago and up and left. We never knew whether she was fleeing old age or bolting for a new life. Contact would be postcards, about as frequent as the ones we got from Laurence, and just as cryptic. That was 10 years ago. Four cards a year, besides Christmas, so 50 cards total perhaps. St. John's, Saint John, Schefferville, Timmins, Thunder Bay, Lloydminster, Medicine Hat, Banff, Victoria. Sometimes a note about a "friend" who was riding with her, once about a stray cat she'd adopted that had torn up the fabric of the seat in the Winnebago's galley. My mother never mentioned my father in those notes, hardly talked about him when she stayed with us. Yet it was hard for any of us to escape my father's influence. I was my father's son; controlling, a know-it-all at times, not always patient, not always kind. Too much oak for this acorn. But unbound by the life he'd defined for her, my mother was living a thesaurus of words for freedom. She was gone, she was unfettered, she was footloose.

I would ask, some evening over a cassoulet at the house on the South Shore, "Mom, where you going next?" And she would answer she didn't know. But you knew she was thinking about it. Every day on the road was a day of decision-making. She made the decisions my father would have made. She set the course and the speed. And she didn't stop for bridges. She could decide to stay an extra night in Moncton — although God knows why — or on her way toward Quebec bypass La Malbaie and stop in St. Irénée. These decisions were all about the future. My grandmother, on the other hand, had already answered the doorbell and discovered death holding out a wrist bouquet for her. She lived day to day. She joked about death, had made peace with her prom date.

The point was ... oh, fuck the point. I was not moving on this accursed bridge and neither, according to the

radio, was the jumper (nor the father for justice, or whoever it was) acting on his threat. The traffic was chipping
away at the chunk of time that I had built for my fabricated errand. We had to get moving soon. We had to. I
could not be late for Laurence. After all these years,
whatever Bijou and I had done to force her to leave home,
I could not insult her, hurt her, by not being there as she
stepped off that Air Transat flight.

The Monday after I first slept with Bijou I found myself facing a rather different kind of standstill.

"I feel we're not moving forward in our relationship,"
Louise said, after another game of foreplay.

"Why can't it be the way it was when we were younger?" I said. "It was free and loose."

We were head to toe having just performed some sex-
ual calculus.

"But we decided we didn't like that. Remember? You
were incredibly jealous when I went out with Norman."

Ah, yes. "I thought I was incredibly high. ... And in any
case, I don't know what you mean by our not moving forward." I rose on my elbows to look at her. "You want to
get married?"

She must have sensed that I blanched as I realized
what I'd just said. It was a question, not a proposal.

"We're 19, Michel. I don't want to get married." She
lifted herself up on her elbows. Her skin glistened, her
pubic hair was moist, a thin crucifix on a fragile gold
chain swung between her breasts. Up by my head, a
bracelet hung like a dewy web from her slender ankle.
Louise was the first girl I'd ever seen naked. Her body
told me so much. I could look at her and see her as she
was in the present, what she must have looked like as a

little girl and what she would look like in her 30s and 40s. It was all there in front of me like a painting, complete and panoptic. With Bijou, it hadn't been like that. Bijou had tone, muscle; there was no past, not even a hint of her pregnancy. All I saw was present. I could sense my own sex rising.

"Then, is it the sex?" I asked.

Louise looked down. She grasped me and tugged gently. "No."

I was afraid to ask more questions. I felt like a lawyer then, or, what everybody says about lawyers: that you shouldn't ask a question to which you don't know the answer. And I knew my own answers to these questions. Louise and I had fallen into a pattern of weekend clubbing with friends — Norman and Alex on occasion, and others from Brébeuf— getting a bit of a buzz on, then when the night collapsed around us like a pair of slipped-off jeans, we had oral satisfaction at her house if her parents were out or in her car in the lookout on Mount Royal. I had already decided, without telling her so directly, though maybe this is what she was reacting to, that she was not "it" for me. Maybe this was one reason why we never actually went all the traditional way.

As much as we dug each other, I never felt she got me. I had the open-trapdoor sensation of seeing Louise's life in its entirety, like one of my compositions: the secretarial job she would have for 15 or 20 years, the affair she would have with her boss, quitting her job after being refused the promotion he'd promised, the lonely sag of her breasts and the thinning of the skin on her hands. I would go back over the vision of Louise's life to see if I'd gotten any part of it wrong, like searching for a misplaced rhyme or a clichéd note. But I hadn't gotten it wrong: I wasn't there. The life I'd imagined for her did not include me, which meant the life I'd previously seen for myself was now a white page. I couldn't marry her. I didn't want to marry her. That I remained with her, continued to date her, was indicative of my reliance on my known world, what was safe, comfortable — even though I knew nothing would come of it, even though I knew Louise would be hurt when we would, inevitably, come to an end.

It was 1981. July. Nine months before, Quebec voters in overwhelming numbers told René Lévesque that they were not comfortable with the idea of breaking up with Canada. The following April we gave him another mandate. Fools and dreamers, plodders and schemers. Who among us acts logically?

Louise's tugging had gotten me sufficiently hard. "Forget it, Michel," she said. And she bent down and gave the tip a kiss. Her mouth tarried there. Perhaps she acted out of the same resignation.

My experience that day underpinned "Déshabillé," which I wrote and gave to Bijou and which she loved and craved more of. "Déshabillé," "La Vie est belle," "Je me découvre," "L'Espace entre les mots," "Musique et paroles," "Tendresses" and "La Sainte Vie," she recorded for *Une Autre Fois*, her next album, which came out in 1983, along with three songs she wrote on her own. Bijou knew about Louise, knew what was happening in my life. I was honest with her and, in any case, there was no hiding the undercarriage of the music and lyrics. Even Bijou's own uncertainty was the foundation of "Musique et paroles." In that song, I'd sought to convey equivocation without writing a song no one could stand to hear. Musical ambivalence makes people uncomfortable, so I sought instead to create tension between what the words and music said, to get at the heart of Bijou's indecision. What was there not to be ambivalent about? She was involved with a man 11 years her junior — sometimes 10, depending on the time of the year, we were quick to point out, someone still in college yet an equal, a coworker, someone artistically mature beyond his years. I wanted to recreate the swell and compression of our time and talk together.

I didn't get it right immediately. It didn't come to me like many of the others did, on a platter like cantaloupe wrapped in prosciutto at an Italian wedding. In fact, I didn't even know how to begin "Musique et paroles" until I sat one day listening to the Beatles through headphones and noticed the final measures of their songs. Some ended absolutely without resolution, left the listener hanging sonically, ready for more. Just one more note, one more pitch that says, "That's it, guv." I wished to recreate the same effect, so worked backward from a final note to find the scale in which I heard "Musique et paroles," a scale in which that final note would be its unresolved fifth degree. As for the lyrics, I did what I often did, or do, and that is to tell a story from Bijou's point of view, which after several years had become second nature. I also thought I could add to the tension in the song's timing by pacing the lyrics to land just off the beat, like a couple that is never quite in synch.

With the royalties I received from writing for Bijou's first album, the winter after the disastrous dinner at Magnan's, I left my room down that long hall from the kitchen. I rented my own apartment on the Plateau, a single large room with a loft above the kitchen area on the third floor of a St. Laurent Blvd. apartment block, the main feature of which was the souvlaki restaurant on the ground floor.

My first taste of international cuisine came at Costas' table, vats of tzatziki piled on greasy slabs of gyro meat, onion, tomato and lettuce in thick buttery pita. I furnished my room, like any college-age kid, with a mattress on the floor, brick-and-board shelves, and rock star posters. I placed potted cacti beneath bare windows that bookended the French doors. I had a couple of guitars — the $100 Yamaha my grandmother had given me so long ago — and a new $2,000 acoustic 12-string from a luthier north of Montreal, plus a keyboard-synthesizer I had finally learned how to manipulate. On one shelf above my stereo I had a collection of PlaySkool children's instruments, including a guitar, a primary-colour xylophone and a tape recorder with microphone, items picked up at yard sales on the streets of Montreal.

I wrote the music and lyrics of "Musique et paroles" and recorded myself on my cassette player. But the guitar was too warm, too confident, for the sound. It was Dutoit at Place des Arts, when what I sought was a wistful girl alone with her diary on the toilet at three in the morning. I tried it on the synthesizer, but the textures were too Carole Laure, too Hall and Oates. Already I could see a road down which synthesizers were leading music — so many acts relied on synths, which freed them up to add horns and orchestration and percussion but which ultimately produced a Styrofoam sound. I didn't want that. I wanted what I could hear in my head and I wasn't sure how to reproduce it.

One night Norman dropped by for a couple of beers before we headed out to Le Cheval Blanc, where we were to meet Louise and Norman's new girlfriend. It was his first time over since he'd helped me move in. And that had been months before.

"It's quite the apartment," he said, ducking his head in the one closed-in space, which was the bathroom. "You don't live like a bachelor. *C'est trop propre.* You sure you don't have Louise living here?"

"Louise? No."

He grinned. "Another girl?"

It was my turn to grin.

"Oh, you bastard. Living here? Does Louise know?"

"No, not living here. She's got her own place and, no, Louise doesn't know." I offered Norman an Ex. He plopped himself down on the couch, with his gangly legs spread and the beer in his crotch. I sat on a short stool next to him. I put my beer on the shelf where I kept my turntable. The keyboard was still on.

"So who is she?"

"Ah," I shrugged. "It's no one you've met. In any case, I'm not even sure I know if we're together."

"You mean you don't know or you're not sure you know or don't know? If it's the second, you better check yourself in."

"Well I like her. I've liked her, I think maybe I've loved her since the first time I saw her, and I know she likes me enough, I mean we ... you know ... but I don't know if she's in it for the long-term." Since she hadn't revealed as much to me, how could I reveal it to Norman? It was still so new for both of us.

We took slugs of our beers.

"So why don't you tell her? And what are you gonna do about Louise?"

I shook my head. "*J'sais pas.*" I put the beer down and turned back. I accidentally hit a note on the keyboard, a sol-la-tee clash in the tinny upper registers.

"That sounds like us!" Norman said. He put his beer down on the floor and got up to the shelf to pick up the toy guitar. "Remember when we had a band?" Norman ran his thumb down the thick plastic strings. "You, me, Jimmy, Richard and …"

"Marc. Les Choristes."

"Yeah! Yeah! That's it. Les Choristes! 'We had joy, we had fun'."

I found the melody right away on the keyboard and together we pulled the cobwebs out of our seasons in the sun.

Norman fell abruptly silent and sank into the well of the couch.

"Sorry, man."

He shook me off. "Naw, naw, it's all right." He bent over, reached for the beer and took a swig. "Shit. Was that just, what, six, seven years ago? Seems like a fucking lifetime. *Crisse.*" He put his beer down and sat back into the couch again. He still held the tiny guitar, about a foot long, by the fretboard. He strummed.

"Do that again," I said.

"What?"

"Thrum the guitar again. Just like you did." I faced the keyboard. Norman ran his thumb down the strings again and up rose a timbre such as I'd heard previously only in my mind. I placed my fingers on the keyboard and listened again. I played the chord. I made a couple of tiny adjustments. I played it again. Norman did, too. "OK. OK." I said, perhaps too impatiently. I struck it again and there it was. I had mimicked the child's guitar sound on the keyboard; it was the sound I'd sought for "Musique et paroles." I riffed through permutations of the song's basic chord, found what I believed to be its insides; it sounded the way I heard it in my head. I sang it for Norman.

"Did you just make that up?" he said.

"No, I've been agonizing over it for months. It was only when you picked up that silly guitar that the sound I wanted came to me."

"Wow, man, you just made that up," he said, oblivious to what I'd just said. "Play it again." I did.

"Play some more."

So I ran through a couple of others I was trying out, nothing he would have recognized.

"You should do this for a living, man," he said.

"Buddy, what do you think pays for this apartment? You think I could pay for this on a weekend security guard's pay?" And I realized I hadn't told Norman about my songwriting — not intentionally; but after a year of not going to school together, of divergent lives growing more so (he was working toward a degree in social work now, at the U of M) — it had never occurred to me to tell him, just as I never told my parents, not even Louise, accustomed as I had become to hiding my life from them.

So I told him all that had taken place in the previous year, including how close Bijou and I had gotten. At midnight, a case of 12 dispensed with, Norman looked at the clock. "*Ah, Crisse, les filles!*" But Louise and Guylaine were no longer in the pub when we got there.

Bijou loved "Musique et paroles." Within a week of my playing it for her, she'd booked studio time and we were all there, in an innocuous tan brick building tucked between a tattoo parlor and a Marché Richelieu in Hochelaga-Maisonneuve. The studio took up the entire second floor, reached by a narrow staircase. It was airless and stale; the halls were carpeted up the walls to about three feet, like some creepy lounge, with the only natural light squeezing in from a thin window at one end of the long main hall. Photographs of *les cinqs géants*, Martine St-Clair and Plamondon, Dubois, other stars, other journeymen, hugging engineers, producers and mixers adorned the walls.

We arrived early, to a studio-bought breakfast of doughnuts and coffee. The players were Bijou, Dany Vox on lead, a bass guitarist whom I'd never met, Octavien "Le Massif" Tremblay on fiddle, and 'Ti Gus behind the Plexiglass with his kit, seven years away from his cancer. What did he know? Did he see his future the way Claude had? The way I had? Pascal Germain parked himself in front of the keyboard. They ran through parts of the song and then the song in its entirety three or four times before 11 a.m. I sat in the booth with Tony "L'Aiguille" Courtemanche, watched and listened as he made adjustments or suggested changes. Tony called a break for lunch. A bit after one the last player straggled in. Tony, Pascal, Bijou and I talked and listened to the morning's work while on the other side of the glass the players jammed. A half-hour became an hour became an hour-and-a-half.

"*Merde*," Bijou said. "This is just not happening."

"Shall we just send everyone home?" Pascal asked. "This is eating up the budget."

I said an afternoon session would probably produce what we were searching for. I shrugged. "But it's not for me to say."

Bijou shook her head. "*Une autre fois*," she said. She went back into the room and reached for a set of headphones.

"Fuck that," the bass guitarist said. "What can we possibly do different? We've gone at this and gone at it again. No matter what you do, you're gonna come out with the same shit."

"Bugger off, Jonas," Pascal said.

Bijou looked at me. Her eyes conveyed an almost funereal gravity; the corners of her mouth sank beneath the weight of her disappointment. I could sense her weigh her choices, uncertain about what to do next. "*J'suis très désolé*, Michel," she said.

"*C'est tout*," Tony said. "Pack it up."

Bijou hung her head while Dany and Le Massif clicked open their cases. Jonas went out the door, followed by Pascal and the others. Bijou sat in a metal folding chair in the middle of the room, herself folded over, holding her head in her hands. Her hair hung limply. Tony said he was off to the front office. I waited alone by the controls. The air there was as stale as in the hallways. Ashtrays filled with cigarette butts sat on the board, on top of end tables, on a shelf in a wall unit. On one of the tables stood a mostly empty bottle of 50 with another butt floating in it. I rapped the window with a knuckle. Bijou didn't look up. It seemed we'd burned out and stubbed out any possibility of recording the song. I rapped again. She lifted her head. Her eyes were rimmed red.

"What is it about this song they just didn't understand, Michel? I was so clear about the sound we were looking for. But they just couldn't — I mean, blue is blue. I called blue, they gave me orange." She got up. I wasn't going to argue with her. I thought she'd called lapis lazuli and they gave her sapphire. They were closer than she'd thought. She ran her fingers through her hair. "I don't even think Tony got it and that's odd because they don't call him 'The Needle' for nothing." She sighed. "You know, it's a bit like some of those last sessions with Beaupré. Nothing clicked. *Rien. Nada.* We would go through take after take of these songs and Marcel was after Gus saying he was off beat and 'Ti Gus would get on Pierre's case for straying ahead, then Pierre would yell at me for jazzing up the tune — and they were my tunes to begin with! — and I would insult Beaupré for his politics, which we all knew by then. *O, seigneur, quelle pagaille.*" She was seated again, but at the keyboard now.

We spoke through the glass wall, over the microphones. When we most needed to comfort each other, we were at a remove.

"It's no wonder you broke up," I said. "Quebec's own Beatles couldn't play together."

Bijou turned toward the window. She wore a lighthouse smile. "You know how to run that board?"

"I was watching Tony. I could probably figure it out. You want me to play something back?"

She shook her head. She started in on the opening chord progression, stopped. "Tape," she said. "When McCartney couldn't get along with Lennon, he played songs by himself. I did the same as Beaupré was splitting up. *Je suis indépendantiste*, for crying out loud! I can do this!"

Bijou recorded it solo at the keyboard-synthesizer. It began tentatively, each note deliberated, mulled over, then she began singing, her voice searching for the

proper register, inspecting both ends before she opted
for a default position, and settled, just like the music, in
a middle space, a place of some comfort to soothe, or
perhaps acknowledge, the ambivalence in the story the
lyrics told. She had worked through the previous disappointment, which had bordered on despair, of the
band's not getting the song right. She muscled the feeling
out through her hands and fingers.

When it was released, the first single off *Une Autre
Fois*, it made its way quickly up the charts, thanks to a lot
of cross-over AM and FM radio play. People said they
didn't recognize the voice as Bijou's right away — as with
John Lennon's voice on his last, "(Just Like) Starting
Over" — until halfway through, or even toward the end
of the song. There, with the choices now made musically
and lyrically, Bijou was able to exude the confidence her
fans had always associated with her. In some integral,
elemental way, "Musique et paroles" — my first production credit — was my love song to Quebec, the tenuous
start, the tension, finally capitulation and coming
together. I said as much many years later, in an interview
with the pop music critic at *La Presse*, after Bijou put out
a greatest hits CD, but he'd looked at me so quizzically
that when I rephrased myself, I felt misquoted.

The single gave her a third solo No. 1. It got her a cover
on several magazines: a triumphant sophomore effort. It
landed both of us in a songwriters' magazine, and then
there we were in *Le Journal de Montréal* labelled "Musique et paroles." The article was short and punchy and
alluded to a relationship we never let on to having. There
was a photo of the two of us in the studio, Bijou at the
keyboard and me nearby with a pad of paper and a pen

in my hands. Later in the week, however, there were pictures of us, taken from behind bushes and trees, in her backyard. There were pictures of us, taken from building corners and through car windows, entering and exiting the Hochelaga studio. None of them was particularly inflammatory and Bijou's manager and sometime keyboardist, Pascal Germain, denied what he could.

There was a call from my father.

"*T'es pas sérieux,*" he said. "Is it true what they're implying?"

"You can make of it what you will."

"What does that mean?"

"It doesn't mean anything."

"Is it serious?"

"Is what serious?"

"This relationship. This songwriting thing."

"I've been writing songs for a long time, Pa. I told you it was serious. You wouldn't listen."

"And you're serious about her?"

"Yes."

"She's an older woman, son. Does she have kids? *Est-elle une divorcée? Et les musiciens,* there'll be drugs, sex orgies."

"I'll wear a condom."

Une Autre Fois' climb up the album charts marked the beginning of our relationship with the paparazzi. And the end of Louise.

For a dozen years. And then a call came.

"You were not that hard to look up, Michel. *Tu es un personage, si tu comprends ce que je veux dire.*"

I understood all too well. Between the success of "Musique et paroles" and *Une Autre Fois* in 1983 and 1995,

Bijou and I collaborated on four more albums. We collaborated when we weren't raising Laurence and trying to make a life for ourselves away from the nightlife of Montreal, away from the push push push of the industry, the demands of the recording companies, the album tours, the pop and hiss of flashbulbs. Yes, yes, we agreed with what Bijou's father said when we complained: We wanted this life, we chose this life, we made this life; but we were determined to also have another life. We had survived Meech Lake, we had ignored whatever had been intended by Charlottetown — Bijou had taken me back to the Languedoc for the year. And then 1995 happened.

"Louise. I still recognize your voice."

"You've always had a good ear."

Louise wanted to meet.

At the InterContinental in Old Montreal, we shared a bottle of Châteauneuf-du-Pape. She said she'd pay. Or rather, her uncle's ad agency would pay. Or rather, as it would turn out, in hearings and reports 10 years later, the Liberal Party of Canada would pay. Louise asked me to write a song for the "*non*" campaign. I said I didn't think I could write on demand and besides I was in the middle of a new project for Bijou.

I had not seen Louise since "Musique et paroles" broke the sound barrier. She was the woman her body dictated she would become. Her hair hadn't lost any of its youthful bounce. It was blonde now though, *toute l'année*, and her stylist had done a superb job blending what was with what was wanted. Louise's face wasn't lined at all. No crow's feet, not even a sparrow's. She was 32? Her birthday was in the fall, I remembered. I drew myself back to childhood parties. Yes, it was in September, right after school started, just before the cutoff date; she'd been one of the youngest kids in our class. The woman before me at that table in the Continental exuded confidence and sparkly wit; when her eyes rested on me, I remembered the smoke on the mountain, and recalled a warm pool of adolescent love. She was not-quite-dancer thin and wore a black skirt that flared just above the knees, a thin white cotton-blend blouse that crossed at the chest, and a necklace and earrings of small onyx cubes.

She didn't seem like a woman who heard "no" very often, even if that's the phrase she most wanted to hear when the referendum results came in. "I can pay, Michel, if that's what you're holding out for," she said.

"It's not the money," I said.

She patted my hand. "I didn't mean you would prostitute yourself. I meant I'm not expecting you to do this free of charge. You are the top songwriter in Quebec. Bijou, Isabelle Boulay, Sass, Garou, Lapointe. Céline herself. Quebecers — Canadians — love your work, and pay for your work. Why should we be any different? If you write a song for the campaign you'd be fulfilling a patriotic duty, you could help save our country. ... And I can pay handsomely, if you do choose to prostitute yourself." She smiled broadly. Such straight, white teeth. I'd forgotten.

I slid my hand off the table and put it in my lap. "It's not about money. I —"

She folded her hands, like a communicant, yet as she spoke they spread open again. I didn't recall her as someone who gesticulated while she talked. But then, when we were younger there were always things in our hands.

Beer bottles and soda glasses, all-dressed steamed hot dogs, pencils and notebooks, marijuana cigarettes, magazines and books. Ice cream cones. "It can't be your politics, Michel. I mean, I know Bijou is a nationalist, but I never thought you believed in separation."

I remembered a bench in front of a dépanneur. It was 1974 and construction for the Olympic Stadium was well underway. To get to our destination that day we had had to walk by a construction site. Graffiti screamed across the plywood barrier that kept sidewalk supervisors from watching the work or kids from hurting themselves on the site at night: "FLQ" spray-painted next to five Olympic rings with the one on the furthest right broken off from the others, a blue outline of the province in the shape of *une fleur de lys*. We sat, me with my legs stretched straight out, she perpendicular to me, cross-legged. Vanilla. I remembered how close she sat, how I felt the coolness of her breath, could sense the up and down motion of her breasts.

"You wore yellow," I said.

"— what?"

I'd interrupted her. I hadn't been paying attention. "You wore yellow, all the time. It was your colour." She had had this pair of shorts, a bright sunflower shade, which rode high up her sun-browned legs. It was the late '70s. Above the shorts, a tight camellia-white T-shirt, French-cut sleeves. Yellow flip-flops. Ankle bracelet.

"Yes, I did. It was."

"Now you wear what we all wear. Black."

"It's Montreal."

I'd got it wrong. I had mapped out some vision of Louise's future when I was 19 and I was wrong. I had predicted she'd be out of work because she'd had an affair with her boss. I had her cooking meals out of boxes and drinking Provigo supermarket wine at a small Formica table in some east-end kitchen. But there she was working for her uncle in promotions and communications, with a Liberal Party contract. She had an MBA from UQAM. She had blonde hair, straight white teeth, a hopeful smile, intelligent, bright eyes, and breasts that hadn't yet encountered gravity. And she sat across from me, her mouth open around a spoonful of *crème brûlée*. What else had I been wrong about?

According to Bijou, I was on the wrong side of the nationalist question. This was it, Bijou said, and that *sot de Shawinigan* was not going to keep it from us.

"That 'idiot from Shawinigan'," I said, "is holding this country together. Quebec is in no condition to be separating."

"There you are wrong, *mon chum*; now is the time," Bijou said.

Why our arguments took place at the breakfast table, I don't know. It was on a side of the house that faced north with an eastern window. The light of the sun sneaked in as if it had been out all night. It was such a crisp, cheery room, and normally we lingered there, in our work clothes during the week — jeans, soft shoes, loose tops or sweatshirts; bath-robed on Saturdays over the — . Ah, that was it. The papers. Our fights normally began after a scan of the newspapers. Bijou argued over much of what she read in *La Presse*, so we got *Le Devoir*, which she agreed with but couldn't tolerate because of its intellectualism, and I picked up *The Gazette* to practise the language of my birthplace. I cancelled the subscriptions.

After a week Bijou figured it out and restarted them. And that, like Laurence, like Chrétien and Charest and Bouchard and Parizeau, like my disconnectedness when it came to my father and my relationship with him, was another topic to fight over.

"Now is the time because we are strong. We can speak in French without shame; we can educate our children in French; we can walk down a street in any city in the province and be able to read the signs in the windows of the stores."

"That's what I'm not getting, Bijou. We have all this, we fought for it and got it and what else can we possibly need?"

The Gazette was folded open in my lap to Macpherson's column on the opinion page. The question sounded like one we asked ourselves from time to time. We have a house; we have two cars, two snowmobiles, a home-recording studio, a grand piano, guitars, computers, a hot tub, two cats and a beautiful 17-year-old daughter. And the dog. Almost forgot the dog. What else did we need? The question was one we even asked, in variation, of that same teenager. You've got no curfew, access to either of our cars, a boyfriend we know you've had sex with, a closet full of clothes all paid for, an after-school job that doesn't pay well but it pays, no rent to pay like some of us did, and you want to do *what*? I folded the paper again and placed it on the table. I looked at Bijou. In those other permutations of the question I myself had just asked her, I got my answer. Independence. I understood that.

My gentle, slow slide into disillusionment and disbelief must have been extremely difficult for Bijou to deal with. She knew what I felt about the PQ government, how it had failed us time and again, reneged on its promises, brought us through 40 years of wandering the desert only to abandon us on the edge of Canaan, our milk and honey limited to bigger letters on storefront signs, the absence of a few apostrophes and the smug satisfaction of seeing English schools close.

"You weren't born here, you didn't grow up here, your parents left Quebec when this province was still run by small-minded, pedophile priests and political lemmings," Bijou said.

This time, we were on the porch, eyes fixed on a place across the river. Félix the Lab had found a ball in the tangle of exposed roots of a tree near the water. The sun was setting behind a low tumble of clouds, yet the sky above was still light blue. Bijou would have said these were the colours upon which Quebec had based its flag. I would have said, yes, but look at the brilliant red underlining the clouds. The picture is not complete without all the colours. "You don't know what it was like for a woman, like my grandmother or my mother, for example, an artist, a respected, admired photographer, to walk into a store and be looked down on as if she were no more than a chambermaid."

"Oh, no, not the Eaton's lady again. No one has ever been able to produce her, you know."

Bijou blew her hair out of her eyes. "You are a writer! You work with metaphor. Even if the story weren't literally true, it has an emotional truth to it, it has a greater ... a bigger-picture truth to it. And that's what we're dealing with here. The truth. Who owns the truth owns the definition. And only Québécois have the right to define that truth in this province. English Canada has never cared, has never bothered to understand it, so they can't bloody define us."

"Yes, but —"

"*Oui, mais, oui, mais, c'est tout ce que tu as à dire!*"

It wasn't all I had to say, it was all I had to say at that moment because from there I knew the argument would descend into some cave in calcified stances until one or the two of us broke off a stalactite for use as a spear: "your mother," "your father," "your youth," "your hard-headedness," "your ambivalence."

In early October, just before the referendum, we celebrated my father-in-law's 70th birthday at a Mexican restaurant in Old Montreal. Bijou's brother berated me, quietly at first but increasingly heatedly. "Have another marguerita, Ange. Calm down."

"*You* calm down, fucking Boy Scout."

After I finished my fajita and an hour of being derided as youthfully ignorant, I excused myself and went outside onto St. François-Xavier Street. The night was crisp. There was a play at the Centaur up the street, *The Stone Angel*. I didn't plan to see it. Margaret Laurence's novel had been enough. A mother looks back on 90 years of stony relationships, never able to properly demonstrate love for her sons. When I'd read it for high school English class, I'd made easy transference to my father. I didn't think the adaptation to the stage would divert so much from the original that I wouldn't relive my own pain.

The door opened. Ange-Aimé stepped out, his left hand shielded his right as he lit a cigarette. He took a drag, exhaled. He turned slightly and noticed me. He marched the four steps to me and stuck his face near mine. He stabbed toward my chest, with the cigarette tucked in the crevice between his first and second fingers. I prayed that my own angel, Bijou, would come out, too, to come between her brother and me, but she remained inside, while I stonily stomached Ange-Aimé's verbal jabs. "You know what always bugged me about you?" he said. He had another drag, so angry he smoked the cigarette almost to the filter, then yanked it out of his mouth and flicked it into the street. It landed in a skid of embers and went black.

"As wet behind the ears as you are, you think you're the one who's going to dry ours, teach the rest of us. But you know squat. And regardless of your family name, you're an anglo, a fucking anglo. Your choice of movies, your choice of books, the music you listen to, the music you write with all the American pop allusions. *T'es pas Québécois.*" He pulled open the door and spat onto the sidewalk before he went back inside.

Louise seemed to be waiting for me to speak. "I believed," I said. "At one time."

"You believed, we believed, in a Quebec free of colonial, religious strictures," Louise said. "That was what we were singing about on the mountain."

She remembered, too, then. I smiled. I rubbed a finger in the corner of my eye, pretending a lash had got loose there.

True to her word, Louise paid for lunch. I got up and pulled her chair back for her. As she turned, she laid her right hand on mine. I didn't pull it away this time. Not immediately. She stepped away. After a moment, I followed. She went to the front desk. I sat in a chair in the lobby. I watched people, singles, couples, small parties, glide up the escalator, or hustle down the stairs. Down the stairs: That's where I needed to go. Down the stairs and around the revolving door into the October light. I needed to get along with my life, not going over the past nor thinking about the life I hadn't lived, the love I had let go. Yet, what was my life right then? I hadn't written new material for Bijou in five years; we were exhausted from worry about Laurence and fighting over the referendum. My wife said I sounded like my father every time I opened my mouth with pronouncements about Quebec.

I saw that Louise had caught an elevator. She held a button to keep the doors open. She tilted her head just slightly and I rose from my seat. I followed her into the elevator and the doors closed and we rose together. I followed her to her room, where we made love for the first and only time, and I showered and left via the elevator and the escalator and the door that opened out onto the mall, where I became lost in the shuffle of shoppers.

"What's that you're working on?" Bijou asked. "It doesn't sound like anything I've heard before." It was about a week after I'd betrayed her trust. "It sounds like a jingle."

"It is a jingle," I said. I was at my keyboard. I had a pencil gripped between my lips. There were sheets of paper on the floor, in my lap, on a table at my side.

"*T'es pas sérieux*," Bijou said. "*Tu fait de la publicité pour qui?*"

"The Liberal Party of Canada," I said.

"You just don't know when to quit do you, you shit." She stomped upstairs.

It wasn't a jingle. What Bijou heard was the intro to a song I called "Le Funambule." I was looking for an opening hook similar to that in Three Dog Night's "The Show

Must Go On" but less circus-like. I didn't know why I had said it was a jingle. I wasn't kidding when I'd said it. And I wasn't even kidding when I'd said the jingle I wasn't writing was for the Liberal Party. I had deliberately set out to hurt my wife. More than that, my weapon of choice had been the very thing with which I'd won her in the first place, 15 years before.

We bickered, we fought, we scratched with words constantly — except for turning a deaf ear or shooting sharp looks, what other slings and arrows do we have but words? But these had been squabbles — over house-keeping; over Laurence and whether our choices and actions had pushed her to leave; over unresolved issues with my father — that had gone beyond argument into domestic white noise. Never had I delivered a punch so purposefully, so accurately, so maliciously as I'd done just then. And I'd never felt so guilty or conflicted either, Louise and the hotel still so fresh. Why had I told her that? What was I thinking?

I took the pencil out of my mouth and dropped it on the pile of papers. I went to my couch and lay down. I was determined to find a physical space where I could work out the emotional state I was in and the couch was usu-ally the place for that. Having let Louise happen, could I now forget her? Was I obliged to write something for her? I had never promised. I had even said as I left the room that afternoon that I would not do it, I could not do it. But if I did not do it, if I didn't write the song, would it ... well, of course it wouldn't. One song couldn't change the course of history.

I fell into sleep and dreamed about Claude's death, but from a cinematic perspective, a point of view very clearly his. I see his eyes when he's running backward, back toward the barn, turning around and about to shout out to his mother: "It's alright, ma, I'm just closing the door." But his eyes aren't looking at his mother at all, they're looking through her, they've shattered the panes of glass in the kitchen window with a glimpse of the future, as if what Claude saw in that millisecond was more than what his small body and soul and eyes could bear, and he cracked.

Everything did crack, the house, his mother, the future. It affected me, too, as a childhood injury would, like a herniated disc or a broken finger that never set right. These injuries never go away; they remind you of their presence continually. And if it's a substantial injury, then it's a substantial reminder. When that childhood injury makes itself known to me, knocks on the door of my subconscious, I see what Claude saw running back to make sure the cows wouldn't get loose, and what he saw was something like what Lévesque saw the night the PQ beat Bourassa's Liberals. He saw the future. Lévesque saw himself perhaps as Moses with the realization this was as much as he would be able to deliver. Or Alexander Herzen, who came to know he and his comrades could but build the bridge of Russian revolution. Others would be the ones to cross it. Claude's eyes were Lévesque's eyes and Lévesque's eyes were those of a haunted man.

There were a dozen haunted eyes glued to television sets the night of the referendum. Bijou had invited two other couples, including Pascal and his new wife, Jasmine, to the house for dinner and then a night of watching the returns. My work for the soirée began the night before when I tossed two cups of borlotti beans into a pot for an overnight soaking. The morning of the referendum, Bijou and I went to vote at the school.

"I don't know why we bother," she said in the car on the way.

"What do you mean?" I said. "It's our responsibility, not just our right." I didn't push the democracy lesson too far, as I knew what she'd meant.

"We'll cancel each other out."

"You don't know that."

"Yes, I don't know. What are the beans for?"

"You like them? Borlotti beans. I like the colour."

"I didn't notice."

"Red and white."

"Bastard."

"I'm serving borscht for a starter. With a maple-leaf shaped dollop of sour cream in the middle."

"Bastard."

"A salad of shredded radicchio, a tart Macintosh apple, some pecans with a creamy buttermilk dressing."

"Mmmmm. But you're still a bastard."

"The main course is a surprise."

"Dessert?"

I took my eye off the road for a quick shit-eating grin at Bijou. "Cherry Jell-O mold with mini-marshmallows."

Bijou collapsed in the passenger seat and we laughed the rest of the three-minute drive to the school. I couldn't remember the last time we'd laughed like that. We held hands as we walked into the polling station. I had a good vibe about the vote.

The main course surprise was osso buco. After voting, I dropped Bijou off at home and drove into St-Jean-sur-Richelieu to my favourite butcher, who had readied for me a dozen shanks of milk-fed lamb. I bought the rest of the vegetables and herbs at an outdoor market nearby and picked up several six-packs of Blanche de Chambly and Maudite, from Robert's company, Unibroue. Mid-afternoon I began assembling my *mise en place*. Then I dusted the shanks and seared them, fried the onion with carrots and some cracked fresh rosemary, the piney scent rising in the mist. The shanks over the vegetables, some tomato purée over the shanks, with seasoning and the Blanche beer to cover. I brought the mix to a boil then lowered the heat to a gentle simmer.

Downstairs in the studio, Bijou was at work. There were periods of quiet followed by series of chord progressions. The chords were hot. Whatever it was, I could sense anger.

From the top of the stairs, I called: "We're not having Jell-O for dessert, Bijou. I don't mean to disappoint you."

Silence, though not the silence of someone writing.

"We're having sour cherry pie and French vanilla ice cream."

More like the silence of someone who'd just stopped writing.

"I thought you'd like that." I waited.

"Go away. I'm writing."

While the lamb simmered in the beer, I made my soup. I added the beans, some herbs and poured more beer onto the lamb. Less than an hour later our guests arrived and Bijou came upstairs to serve the cheese with the Blanche. The lamb was falling off the bone. On another burner, I boiled water for polenta. We were six of us in the kitchen, against the countertop, propped against the refrigerator, on stools at the centre island. I never left my stove-front post.

"Did you hear about Céline?" Pascal said. "Phil Spector."

"She's dumped René?" I joked.

"As producer?" Bijou asked.

"Apparently he saw her do 'River Deep, Mountain High' on TV and wanted to produce her next album," Pascal said.

"You mean control her next album," I said. I added some cooking cream and grated Parmesan with freshly ground pepper.

"I love *D'eux*. Don't you think it's a great album? Have you heard 'Vole'?" someone asked. It was Marguerite, one-half of the other couple. She and Bijou had known each other at the National Theatre School. It was Marguerite who had introduced Bijou to Leon Russell's "Superstar" long ago and oh so far away.

Later that night the song would come back to me. "Don't you remember you told me you loved me, baby?" Early in the evening, the *bavardage* in the kitchen seemed easy. But it's possible the cooking distracted me.

"Who hasn't heard *D'eux*?" I asked. "It's everywhere. Can't turn on the radio without hearing it. There'll be a referendum in 10 years, we'll still be hearing it."

"But we're not bitter, are we?" Jasmine said.

"The beer's not bitter at all," said Marguerite's husband, Jonathan, an older man, going deaf I suspected. "It's got a nice sweetness to it."

"Dion's no Tina Turner," I said, to Pascal.

"She's got legs," Jasmine said.

"Not Turner's legs," I said.

"But 'Vole' is such a nice song, about her niece who died of cystic fibrosis," Marguerite said. "And 'Pour que tu m'aimes encore' is dynamite."

"John Turner's planning a comeback?" Jonathan said.

"No, sweetie," Marguerite said. She patted his hand.

"Neither's Ike," Pascal said.

"*Approchez-vous*," I said and took the *soupière* out to the dining room.

"Where's Laurence?" Marguerite asked.

"Spain," Bijou said quickly, though we knew otherwise.

"Blowing up the charts in France," Pascal said. "It's been, what, five or six months now? *D'eux*'s still No. 1. Céline's doing it right."

"Right place, right time," I said.

"Right songs," Bijou said.

I shot her a look.

The others must have seen it. Certainly they'd heard it. Pascal looked at Bijou, then at me. He went back to his soup.

"So what about Spector?" Jasmine asked.

"He quit," Pascal said. "Walked into the studio, got a load of grief from her handlers and buggered off."

"I can't believe that," Marguerite said. "He walked out on Céline? Who does he think he is?"

"Shakespeare," Bijou answered.

I brought out the osso buco and polenta and placed it in the centre of the table.

"Red and white soup; red and white salad ... have you turned into a Liberal?" Pascal asked. "We'll fire you now if you have," he added, pointing a fork at me but unable to hide a full-cheeked smile.

"We had a blue cheese," I said. "I'm an equal opportunity cook. And the lamb was from Quebec."

"Really?" Marguerite asked. "At this time of the year?"

"Quebec's production of lamb is year-round," I said.

"Phil Spector produced the Wall of Sound," Jonathan said, finally coming around to the earlier discussion.

" 'Round,' Jonny," Marguerite said. "We get lamb year-round."

"And the beer is—"

"Quebec, too," I said.

"You're just a regular Quebecer, aren't you?" Bijou said.

She got up and went into the living room to turn on the television. It was well after seven. Polls closed in half an hour and results would trickle in shortly afterward from les Îles-de-la-Madeleine and Manicouagan, the homes of the most ardent of nationalists, the inspiration for so many of Beaupré's songs, where one could walk seven days in any direction and not hear Russian or Portuguese or Italian or Hebrew or Arabic or Spanish or Greek or English and not see anything but our national colours, blue, white (and green). We followed Bijou into the living room and sat around the television in our Quebec house with our Quebec beers and watched Quebec disintegrate. As the early returns filed in, I recalled another election, another set of families, another television.

It was 19 autumns earlier. The Olympics were over. The United States had just elected a peanut farmer as president. There were six Canadians in the Top 30, if you included Paul Anka, who had to remind people he was not from Las Vegas. Boule Noire had begun a disco-inflected R&B career with his debut album, *Aimes-tu la vie*. Pagliaro had another album in English. Its second single, "I Don't Believe It's You," was charting after "What the Hell I Got" — and some people were confused about the hell it was they had. They must have been confused to have not seen the possibilities embodied in the Parti Québécois.

My father spent a good chunk of October and November ranting against Bourassa for calling an election two years early and based on the success of the Montreal Games. "*Retardé*," my father called it. "What does he expect? A gold medal? Maybe for idiocy." Nonetheless, he spewed what venom he had on Lévesque and the "*Parti qui soit*," which was his way to say the PQ was a party of one, the godlike Lévesque, He Is Who Is. When election night came around, my parents sat around the television with my aunt and uncle and my uncle's sister and her husband, who were Norman's parents. My father told us to run off, but I insisted we watch.

"It's my country, too!"

"Your country. I'll give you 'your country'."

"Raising a little *indépendantiste*, Noël?" my aunt, Marie-Madeleine, said.

"He's just doing it to be a rebel," he responded.

"Am not! This is the best thing that could happen to the province. '*On a besoin d'un vrai gouvernement*'."

The adults broke out in a laugh.

"Well, we know he can read the advertisements," Théophile, Norman's father, said.

I shrugged and went to the kitchen with Norman until the start of the returns.

The three men went through a case of Ex that night, and grew angrier as the night went on.

"It's on again!" I called out to Norman, more stage than whisper. We sat on the floor behind the couch, in the area that was neither living room nor dining room, unable to see the TV but able to hear the announcer as he called in the returns and introduced reporters in various campaign headquarters. I handed him the earphone and my transistor and we passed it back and forth to hear Rod Stewart one more time. "Tonight's the night," I sang.

"How could he have done this?" my father said. I peeked over the back of the couch. He'd jerked up and faced the television. He looked ready to kick it. "How could he have called this election?"

"Noël, sit down," my mother said. "We can't see."

He sat. "What the hell are they thinking?" he asked, as the province's ridings slid one by one into the Péquiste column.

Norman asked no one in particular, "Are we going to have to move to Ontario?"

"No, sweetie, we're not moving to—"

"Ontario?" my father said. "Who's moving to Ontario? You'd move to Ontario? You're a Quebecer!" As the night progressed, he got shriller, as if the alcohol had cut out all the bass.

"Noël, *calme-toi*," my mother said.

"Spread your wings and let—" I sang.

"Will you shut that thing off?" my father bellowed.

"Leave him alone," my mother said. "He doesn't even know what he's singing."

"All the worse," he answered.

Bourassa was on the screen. My father stood. "*Câlice d'enfant d'chienne*," he shouted.

"Everything's going to be different, isn't it?" Norman said. "Everything's changing."

"Noël, sit."

"Nothing will change, Norman," his mother said.

My father sat.

"It's the Union Nationale," Théo said. "They've split the vote."

"Union Nationale," my father said. "Liberals. Bourassa. All to blame."

"There was no way Bourassa could win," Théo said.

"Péquistes win and we move," my father said. "I swear to God we're moving back."

"You just returned," said Christian, Marie-Madeleine's husband.

"Oh, hell," my father said. "They'll rule with a minority government and won't be able to do shit."

"That's not a minority government," Christian said. "Sixty, seventy seats, whatever they get tonight is a majority."

"A majority of nothing. They've got no mandate. Forty per cent of the people? That's not a majority."

"No, but it's enough."

"Everything *is* going to change. I know it."

"Gonna be alright ..."

"Will you shut that fucking thing off?!"

I looked up, as my father reached over the back of the couch with his arm. He clutched wildly at my head and earphone. I ducked, scrambled and raced out into the hall. "Get back here!"

"Misha!"

I was yanked back.

"Can you be here when I'm talking to you?" Bijou said.

"What?"

We were in the bedroom. It was after midnight and Pascal, Jasmine, Marguerite and Jonathan were 15 minutes into their drives home.

"You were quiet tonight," she said. "It didn't seem like you were all here. Like a wall had descended on you."

"I had a fright," I said.

" 'A fright?' " she said. "Is that what you call it? A major disappointment is more like it." She had pulled off her sweater and was undoing her bra. "This is the saddest day of my life."

"After all I cooked for you?"

"Ha ha. You know damn well what I mean." She slipped her pajama gown over her head and pulled the end down over her pants, then pulled the pants down and stepped out one leg at a time.

"I'll tell you what I didn't know." I threw my shirt into the corner near my bureau.

"Will you pick that up?"

"I'll put it in the laundry tomorrow."

I sat on the edge of the bed and took off my socks and pants and underwear. Tossed them into the corner, too.

"Honestly," she said.

"What's the big deal?"

"You know what the deal is."

"Is this about the laundry? This isn't about the laundry, is it?" I turned.

Hands on hips, she shook her head.

"It's not about the referendum either, is it? As bad as that was for you. As much as our votes cancelled each other out."

Again, she shook her head.

"Laurence? Are you mad that I gave her the money to go on the student exchange?"

Not that either. "We all wanted it."

"It can't be about Céline. You're not jealous, are you?"

She shook her head again. "As much as I can't stand it, I don't begrudge the woman her success. She came by that honestly."

I stood and faced her. "Then what the hell is it? Because I'll tell you what's been bugging me."

"What. What's been bugging you? What could honestly be bugging you? You got your 50 plus one."

Yes "my" side won, but I hadn't gloated, not at all. Yet here we argued still, an hour after the results were public. I knew I should have been more gentle with her; I knew how much this loss meant. Yet I could not say the words. She was upset with me, but not about the vote. The tone of the argument was the referendum, but the vibrations ran deeper than that.

"The referendum isn't what's bugging me," I said. "It's what you said about Céline having had the 'right songs.' What kind of dig at me was that? What were you trying to say? I don't write well enough for you anymore? You're not happy with what I'm writing?"

"Céline Dion isn't the problem."

"Then what is it, for Christ's sake?"

"A little bird happened to see you in the InterContinental Hotel a couple of months ago."

"Shit," I said, mostly to myself. I had stood on my side of the bed so many times, talking, pulling down the sheets to slide in with Bijou, almost always naked, sometimes hard as she crawled to my side and sucked me or slid herself over me and we made love standing, but never had I felt so completely exposed. The blood drained from my face and my hands and arms went numb.

"The little bird said you were with someone. A blonde. And you had lunch. And after lunch you took a room. And you didn't leave the hotel for several hours."

"Honey ..."

"Don't."

"Honey, I ... It was one time. I don't know what happened. I just — I love you, Bijou. It's—"

"You bastard. You think I care that you went off and fucked someone in the fucking InterContinental Hotel? I know you love me. Fuck! You bastard! You were with Louise Pelletier! You slept with your ex-girlfriend and she gave you a contract to write music for the 'No' side. You wrote advertising songs for them to help turn the referendum. You lied to me!"

"I didn't write anything. I didn't. I swear I didn't."

"You liar. You told me you were. When I asked you what you were writing that day, when I said it sounded like an advertising jingle you said that's exactly what it was. You said it was for the Liberal Party."

I had never told her it was a joke. As absorbed as I was in the referendum and the discord between Bijou and me, guilty as I had felt for the previous two months about Louise, and even though she must have heard me continue to work on "La Funambule," she never had cottoned on to the fact that there was no jingle emanating from my guitar or keyboard.

"Bijou, it was a joke! I write for you. You're the only one I write for. I've always written just for you — to seduce you, to impress you, to humour you."

She started to cry. "That's not true."

I had to try levity. I felt a need to end the discomfort, diffuse the situation. I was wrong to sleep with Louise. I knew I was wrong then, and I'd done it. And I knew I was wrong now and I'd apologized. But it was a song — a jingle — that had upset Bijou and of that crime I knew I was innocent. "You're right. There was Sass and Johanne and Isabelle and Marjo."

"And Paul and Richard and Claude. And Louise!" She sobbed. "Dammit, Misha, if you were able to write all those songs for me, these songs in which I felt such connection, in which I believed you really understood me and, yes, that impressed me and seduced me, and then you turn around and write a jingle, a lousy jingle for Chrétien and his Shawinigang, how then can I believe you've ever known me, ever known who I really am and what is important to me?"

I collapsed on my knees on my side of the bed. "I didn't do it, Bijou. I didn't. I admit I had sex with Louise. And for that I am deeply shamed and very sorry. But I did not betray you." It was my turn to cry. I cried the tears of a man clinging to all he holds dear, a man wrongly accused, a misunderstood boy. I cried tears I should have cried at other times. I felt a weight on the bed. Bijou had slid over. She cradled my head in her arms.

"Why, Misha? Why?"

But I couldn't tell her. I could not confess I'd wanted to hurt her, admit that I still held Bijou accountable for Laurence's running away.

My tears subsided. I wanted the music to return, but it was gone.

How would Claude have voted in 1995? And what type of man would he be now? I often asked myself. Would he have married, had a child or two? What kind of education would he have had? Would he work with his hands? Would he have made it to the city? Would we still be friends? Would we like the same music? Back before we had the technology to burn CDs, I would make tapes titled Claude I, Claude II, one per year from the time I got a tape recorder, some time after he had died, my way to fish out, through music, where I was at that moment. The new CD I'd burned for Claude I kept it in the car, in the glove compartment. This latest one, which I slid into the player while I was stuck on the Jacques Cartier Bridge, was numbered Claude XXV. My eyes filled. That was partly the Charles Aznavour. "Hier encore" could do that to anyone. Who doesn't think he hasn't wasted his life? Or, at least parts of his life. And then I wondered, well, have I? I loved my life. And I loved the music (Claude and) I listen to: Bijou (obviously), Aznavour's "Emmenez-moi," Jools Holland, Steve Earle, Les Colocs, Sleater-Kinney, the original Fleetwood Mac, Serena Ryder, Johnny Cash, Feist, KT Tunstall. That's what I put on this disc. It fit into 80 minutes.

And yet it wasn't enough. All the disc really says is "this is what I hear." It doesn't convey the story of my life, the emotional current that runs through it. As hard as it is to admit, as a songwriter, perhaps music *can't* communicate every feeling and thought and action — perhaps music isn't the template for all of life after all. I stopped working on "La Funambule." I abandoned music. When Bijou asked, I said I was thinking.

I spent the year after the referendum wishing Laurence would come home, that I could return to a life with Bijou, that I could learn to bridge the distance between us, go back to a time when the connection was stronger. But for that, I would have had to change the past, and that is a stream no man can swim. The least one can do is study that which came before — the people and places, the fading-away faces — like studying the current of a slow-moving river. Then, when one is ready, make the plunge. Still, the river is never as slow as it looks when you fly above it.

The Chicoutimi River, or any of the Saguenay-area rivers that flooded during the summer of 1996, the Ha! Ha!, the Mars, aux Sables, were quick to anger and sluggish to recede. They were not unhurried from any vantage point. Perched aboard a Canadian Forces helicopter, guests of the commander at the CF Bagotville base, Bijou and I toured the flood-struck areas.

I hadn't wanted to go. She'd insisted. I think I would have been happy to just watch RDI and then write a cheque. Instead, with a pilot and his assistant, we flew over Grande-Baie, Chicoutimi, Jonquière, Ferland, Boilleau, Laterrière, Bagotville, L'Anse Saint-Jean, Rivière Eternité, and Petit-Saguenay. We passed over the Kenogami and Ha! Ha! lakes, odd spots of blue muted by brown. All types of brownness: bark brown, cardboard brown, 70-per-cent chocolate brown, lentil brown, the brown that passes as red in brick, and the brown that passes through a very sick man. We saw the gold statue of Jesus with his arms stretched out as if seeking to ascend into the helicopter, a lift-up, an evacuation, a way to rise above the death and destruction about him. The cataract just behind, 10 metres of cascading menace flowing from the spillover of Chicoutimi's Pont-Arnaud dam, poured down Rue Gédéon — and what would that good judge say now? Probably what he says every time one opens Judges: where are you, God? where are your wonderful works? — and flooded the cemetery behind Sacré Coeur Church. The sodden earth loosened and flowed away. It took with it more than a few of the cemetery's otherwise permanent residents. The notes that announced Judgment Day had sounded, but the alarm was early. Coffins shoved against the wall of the church.

We saw trees stripped of branches and scattered like toothpicks on the floor of a diner. We saw railway ties upended vertically like ladders, a bridge folded like a plastic straw into the Ha! Ha! River. We saw a tractor-trailer and mobile homes — a good 30 of them — floating sideways and upways and whichways like a logjam in a newly formed lake in the deepest interior of Quebec. The lake was stocked with the dead, like sea kayaks set adrift. Everything we saw we had to liken to something else to understand it, but to do so made it less than it was. Everything we saw was so beyond our experience, our emotional range, our capacity to comprehend. We were compelled to search for metaphors. It was like trying to discern God. It was like trying to fathom what Claude saw in the moment before he died, or what Lévesque saw as he lifted his arms and tried to quiet the expectant crowd. All that destruction, all the stuff of all those lives, old lies and new truths, now flotsam and jetsam.

"This river used to be my street," said the helicopter pilot, Alan, a young captain, just out of the Université du Québec à Chicoutimi. "That's my house there." I could hardly hear him and his co-pilot, Robby, over the noise of the blades above and the roar below. Clean-shaven with a downturned smile, he pointed. His voice rose when he said "there," and when he pointed and he said "that's my house there," we looked, but there was no house there. The home was three years old, he said. Two storeys, four sides of aluminum siding, a couple of doors, and a dozen windows — and every memory and butter knife contained within — had slid off the concrete foundation like a child down a waterslide. Except there was nothing to catch that young house, and the water that had given that house the shove filled in the foundation, for nothing fills a hole like water. Alan pointed and we stared. Then Bijou put her hand on his shoulder and he dropped his arm and it was his turn to stare. "Thank you for coming here," he said. "This will mean a lot to the people, who have lost everything. This means a lot."

"Let's go down," Bijou said.

"Good idea," I said.

Bijou turned and looked at me, for having spoken for the first time on the trip I suppose. She smiled, then turned back to Alan.

"If you want to," she said.

He looked at her with uncomprehending eyes, shook his head. Did he not think it would help him psychologically, emotionally, to see what remained of his house? Was he not ready? Or were we just too thick to see that the chopper's rotor blades might catch in downed electrical power lines while we tried to navigate our descent — and this was too much of a risk for the pilot to make with a high-profile Quebec singing star aboard? *"Pas tout d'suite,"* he said. On second thought, I couldn't have agreed more, not right now. Perhaps not ever.

We were quiet. I looked out the chopper's window. Below us the river raged, white water sluices indicated the presence of an obstruction that had somehow resisted the pressure to move on. Everywhere I looked: the same. There was no end to the water and the damage done. One could no more make out the end than see the other side of the Gulf of the St. Lawrence. One knows there's another side. Alan had seen what he'd needed to see of his future, it seemed to me. Because it was not just fattened family photo albums, coasters and memories that had floated away, it had been the future, that unsee-able side on the other side of the horizon. He would maybe have said there's no point trying to salvage a fu-ture when all you have salvaged, all you have to build on, is a streaked photo of *ma tante Adrienne* and a splintered door jamb. I felt like saying but didn't — it was too soon and too trite — that when the rage subsided, he would find the ability to move on, he would find the strength to build his future. Right now, he had the strength to fly a chopper and shake his head.

A flash of light caught my eye on the way back to Bagotville. We circled over an area just south of Lac Ken-ogami that was polka-dotted with islands of various sizes and greenness, like isolated tussocks in the tundra of a melting Canadian Arctic.

"I saw something," I called. "A flash."

"I saw it, too," Alan said. "I'm going to turn around. It may have been just some kind of reflection. But let's see."

It was no reflection. Hovering over a recently created islet, we could see clearly three people, a man and two women, or a woman and a girl. The man shining the mir-ror toward us waved frantically.

Alan, in the pilot's seat, raised his hand in salute.

"There somewhere to drop?" Alan asked Robby, who was about the same age as his boss but quieter, more in-tense. He shook his head.

"*Est-ce que c'est possible*? What are they still doing out there?" I asked.

Bijou touched my arm. She put a finger to her lips.

"I don't want to risk going down there," Alan said.

"Fine," Robby replied. "I'll set up the sling."

"No, no, wait. Hold on," Alan said. He found an opening and we dropped steadily down to less than a foot above the ground. Robby slid open the side door. The deafening whop-whop of the blades replaced the beat of our hearts. Robby fastened himself with a belt and hook near the open side door of the helicopter, then stood, one foot on the landing gear. Bijou turned in her seat. I moved into the back and found a belt to hook myself, too. I had no idea why. I felt like I should. Robby motioned to the family to bend down and come to the helicopter.

He reached for the first and pulled her up. The mother tumbled in. Tears streaked her face. "Merci, merci," she said. Then she turned quickly toward the door. "My daughter," she said. "My husband and my daughter — we've got to get them."

Bijou left her seat and sat beside the woman. "*Bonjour*," she said. The woman smiled. "*Asseyez-vous avec moi, ici.*" Bijou motioned to the rear of the chopper, against the wall opposite the door.

"No, no, we've got to get my daughter," the woman said.

"We've got to have room for your daughter to come aboard, ma'am. Maybe it's best," I said, "if you do sit back here. It'll be fine, don't worry. What's your name?"

And she let herself to be taken three feet away toward safety in the womb of the chopper, allowed Bijou to wrap her in a blanket, this woman named Anik. Bijou looked at me over Anik's shoulder. I imagined her soothing Laurence; I saw her the way she'd taken 'Ti Gus in her arms when she saw him at Dany Vox's funeral; even the way she sometimes consoled a fan backstage who fainted at her feet. Although it had been only since November that

I had left the house, I realized how long the eight months had been and how I could not envision an equivalent length of time that would further separate me from her. I was 34. For two-thirds of my life, I had been enveloped in Bijou, her music, her voice, her person, her love. The look told me we were still connected.

A gust of wind forced the chopper up and to the left. Robby slipped. Anik shrieked. I grabbed Robby and helped him up. "Whoa, Alan!" I called.

He righted the helicopter. Once again, the young man was at the door, grasping. "Alan," he shouted. "Let's go for the girl."

"*Vas-y.*"

Below us, the man, wet and tall, held his daughter in his arms. She reached out. Perched on one of the skids, Robby grabbed her at the wrists, I had her legs, and we pulled her in.

"*Maman!*" the girl cried and the woman reached forward with both arms to draw her in and draw her back and draw her into Bijou, who was there for both of them.

Robby and I turned our attention to the girl's father. The chopper moved and Robby could grab him only by the hand and not the wrist like the others. The wind buffeted the helicopter and Alan fought to keep it steady. The man lost his grip and he fell back to the ground. Alan brought the chopper down again. Again, the man tried to climb onto the helicopter's skid but his foot slipped. The chopper roared up. We were now three metres above the angry river with the man hanging on by only his right hand. His legs, like blunted kindergartener's scissors, cut through the air. The movement was too much for the tenuous grip the young co-pilot had on him.

"Jeremy!" the woman behind me called as her daughter shouted: "Daddy!"

A powerful burst of wind jolted the chopper.

And he was gone.

Anik broke free of Bijou and rushed the door. "Jeremy!" she yelled. We watched him float away, wave furiously in one instance and disappear beneath the froth the next, a bob on a fishing line.

Alan turned the chopper around and we raced downstream after Jeremy. Robby was back at the door, with his butt in a sling tied with a nylon-coated steel cord wrapped around a motorized pulley in the ceiling of the chopper. He jumped out. The cord's whirr as he descended suggested to us the speed at which one must travel to meet life.

Bijou took Anik by the shoulders, and shepherded her to the back of the chopper where they sat with the girl, about 11 or so, who whimpered and shivered in the cold.

The helicopter, with Robby trailing behind like a loose shoelace, followed Jeremy to where the waterlogged man was caught on a tree branch. We waited above him. Robby waved and Alan pushed a button to allow his co-pilot to descend a foot or two more. Robby splashed into the river, which rushed around him and his quarry. Robby wrapped the sling around himself and what appeared to be the lifeless body of someone who had been, possibly, a good man, a decent father, impatience not unknown to him, but gentle and firm, and a satisfying lover and husband, tender and forgiving. I couldn't have known that, but the looks of desperation and love and pain and fear on the faces of Jeremy's wife and daughter, sandwiched in the blanket with Bijou, made me think it was possible.

Beneath us, Robby gave an exaggerated wave. Alan pushed another button and the pulley motor clicked. The cord reversed itself and Robby and Jeremy, arms outstretched, legs dangling, ascended.

At Bagotville, Alan and Robby and I carried Jeremy on a canvas Canadian Forces stretcher to the base clinic. He was pale with a tint of blue-green. His face was scratched. Blood seeped through tears in his T-shirt and jeans. There were twigs and leaves in his hair, and he smelled of the putrefaction that was once a bountiful, pleasurable river, a river to vacation on. The hulk of a man we'd seen earlier had been replaced by a frail replica. He breathed shallowly. Aboard the helicopter we'd covered him in the blankets that remained and dried him. Anik had cradled him as he coughed and spit up water.

With the commander later, Bijou and I went over in detail the events of that morning as he made notes. Then we took a tour of the mess hall and recreation centres, which had been converted into a barracks for about 800. "When do you want to head back?" I asked Bijou.

"I don't think I want to right now," she said.

"I don't mean now," I said. "A couple of hours?"

"I mean I don't want to leave today," she said. "I want to stay and work. There must be something we can do here."

We stood at the doorway of the old mess hall. Some lay on green army-issue cots; some sat. Radios here and there. A couple of children played tag. A mother nursed.

"Hey! It's Bijou!" someone shouted.

"Oh, shit," she said under her breath. "I don't need this now."

"Let's go then," I said. "Quick."

But a crowd had formed and a television camera got up close and personal. Bijou lifted her face to the fans, put on her best smile, and entered the room. She shook hands with the men, kissed the women and children, and massaged the cheeks and heads of the babies. She appeared saintly to me then. I didn't say anything afterward. Maybe I should have. She was everything I wanted and loved and had married. When she'd called and told me about the offer to tour the area, I'd said a trip to the Saguenay would be seen as a photo op — "Oh, there's Bijou again, primping for the cameras" — and I'd said she shouldn't do it. That morning before we left, I said it again.

At 44, nearly twice the age of when I had first seen her, Bijou had doubled in my estimation. As unforgiving as my "vision" of Louise's future had been many years before, I couldn't have imagined where Bijou would be now: from the cascade of her hair to the slope of her shoulder and turn of a cheek down the slip of her calf and the pleasure chamber that is the arch of her foot, she was the physical embodiment of grace. Yet that was just a part of this incarnation of goodness and what she meant to me. There was her body, and there was her body of music. How many people had she touched in the intervening years, through her albums, the radio, in concert? Her voice warmed friend and stranger alike, connected people to each other. This was one of the paradoxes of our relationship, I suppose: Bijou was able to touch her fans with words written by me, who remained at a remove.

I was still that young guy who circled around the lawn of Bijou's house for her album launch party. Still the

budding writer who kept secret from his father and
family his desires, what he sought from life. Had I so developed my need for self-protection as a child and teenager that as an adult I found it hard to forge the distance
between myself and others? I never did repair the relationship with my father. But I'd had a close relationship
with Laurence, and Bijou and I were as attuned as twins.
Perhaps I'd allowed the proximity to grow familiar, allowed complacency to saturate our marriage the way
water bloated these Saguenay houses. The night of the
referendum Bijou had said it was the jingle-writing for
the Liberal Party ad — more than my having slept with
Louise Pelletier — that had upset her so. How could I
know who she was and commit such an act of betrayal,
she'd asked. Yet when she asked me to leave two weeks
later, it was the affair, if one can call it that, which she
blamed.

I thought a lot — and wrote, not much, a couple of
tunes for a singer who was about to enter the U.S. market — in the eight months between the referendum and
the floods, and I came to the conclusion I'd allowed the
relationship nearest and dearest to me to slip away.

We peeked in on Jeremy and his family from outside
the door. He was seated on a cot, the grey blanket thrown
over his shoulders. His daughter was next to him, her
head against his shoulder. Anik sat in front of them.
They leaned forward as if gathered in prayer. In his
hands, Jeremy held a piece of bread. His wife ran her
hands in his hair and whispered something. The girl
giggled. He ate some of the bread. Anik handed him a
cup next. He blew into it and brought it to his lips. He
sipped from it, slowly.

Over the next week, the receding water left behind a sweet stench of rot and decay, death's vinegary-vomit pinch, the smell of brownness. The town stank of septic tanks and leech fields. It stank of disease, of rugs and chesterfields left to mildew, of bacteria allowed to grow. Smell that allows no room for the imagination. This is what it is and there's no other word for it. Vinegar and vomit. Can death be reduced to such parts? I was thoroughly disgusted and overwhelmed at the same time with the work that had to be done. We needed to leave.

"There's talk of a concert," Bijou said on the flight home. "I've been asked to sing, to raise money for the flood victims."

"That's good. Some decent exposure, for a good cause."

She named a few singers, most of the invitees being Québécois, but others, Corey Hart, Alanis, English-Canadians with heart. "I'll need you to help me round up commitments. *Ainsi, j'ai juste une autre petite chose à te demander.* I'd like you to write a song for me, Michel. Especially for this concert."

"Bijou." I shook my head.

"For these people," she said.

I closed my eyes and bit my lip.

"But ... I couldn't do this. Look at all we saw—"

"What we smelled."

"Still smell. All that. I couldn't do justice to this."

"Michel, you are the only one who can write this. You have told me and told me and told me that all music comes out of a social context. You said it of Beaupré; that our personal experiences gave rise to our political expression and our political expression was inseparable from our artistic one. Well, this is your social context. This is your opportunity to be personal and political *and* artistic."

I waited. She turned in her seat and faced me. "Misha, I saw something on that helicopter that scared me half to death."

"You didn't show it."

"I did my best. I had Anik in my arms. And her daughter. I couldn't be freaking out."

"I'm glad you didn't."

"Quit interrupting me. You're not making what I have to say any easier."

I was taken aback — didn't know she wanted to say something — but I leaned in toward her in deference and apologized.

"What I saw that scared me half to death was an image of the future, my future, one without you. It was the emptiest place I ever saw. It felt as if I were adrift in the river myself aboard the flimsiest piece of pressboard. I thought I would drown. Then Robby came up with the body of Jeremy and I saw you grab him and swing him into the belly of the helicopter. I saw Anik and their daughter scramble to him and embrace him."

I waited.

"I can't be without you, Misha."

Sometimes you can't be with me, I thought. But I didn't say it. It would have been a cheap comeback, like the night after the referendum when I'd tried to make light of her disappointment. She says she can't live without me. I know I can't live without her. But this won't happen now. It's only been eight months. We need to know. And we will. Just not yet.

I didn't write "Embrasse" for the flood victims. A simple song wouldn't help. Though how did I know that for sure? I hadn't written the "Non" campaign song for Louise. The campaign won anyway. Yet recent musical history was full of songs written for charitable causes, the gun-control campaign in Britain after the massacre of the kindergarteners in Dunblane, for one. Dany Bolduc — perhaps he should have stuck to translating Beatles and the Everly Brothers — had tried to raise funds with the saccharin "St-Jean-Vianney," which remembered the night in 1971 when this Quebec town, lodged on the remnants of a 500-year-old landslide, slid again and 40 homes and almost that many people were lost. Michael Jackson and Quincy Jones wrote their heart-wringing, let's-help-the-starving-people-of-Africa ditty during the Ethiopian famine, yet what happened? A year later, long after the strained voices of Stevie Wonder and Bruce Springsteen had faded away from "We Are the World," the money stopped flowing in, the aid going out was plugged up and people continued to die. With Bob Geldof and Band-Aid, same thing. One song or one concert wouldn't change anything. The question, it seemed to me, was an existential one. I didn't respond to Bijou immediately. I begged time. I needed time. I had questions.

Does one shape the world, or does the world shape us? An old question. The stuff of Plato and Cervantes. In my context, how much power does a song have to change the world? In the end, I wrote it. Writing "Embrasse" for Bijou was another note in the love song I had been writing for her since I was 12, when I caught that first glimpse of her on the cover of the magazine. It would be "Pourquoi non, moi et toi" all over again. I hoped.

Chorus

Faire nourrir,
faire mourir

"Must we listen to this?" my father asked. While he had a glass of beer in the kitchen, my mother set the supper table. My sister was in her room, I was in mine, stretched out on the bed with my homework and the radio on. I heard the rocking chair creak. He'd gotten up. I rose and lowered the volume. I heard the shuffle of his feet as he returned to his place. "How can he do homework listening to that?"

It was probably my mother who finally persuaded him to allow me to buy headphones. It was the first major purchase I made on my own. Previously I'd bought albums and singles, and though they added up to some major coin, singly they were not that expensive. For a week, I studied the circulars in the newspapers and read magazines in the library. I was ready. The next time we went to the mall, I would buy myself a pair of headphones.

The front of the store was wall-to-wall with television sets. I caught a glimpse of the hornbill-nosed premier on the news, then a news anchor filled the screen, and then the challenger, Lévesque. My father stopped in front of a set. "Look at this," he said. My mother stood by him. My sister drifted off to another bank of TVs.

I walked past the televisions and the stereo systems and stereo components and entered a room in the back lined with speakers. A couple were denuded of their black protective baffles to expose the paper-thin tweeter and woofer cones. The headphones were hooked on metal trees. I forgot all I'd read in the circulars and went for the biggest, blackest, cushiest phones. I lifted the phones and slipped them over my head. My pajamas had never felt that comfortable. The phone jacks were plugged into a receiver. I felt a hand on my shoulder. A salesman, about my dad's height but somewhere in his 20s with dark hair below the ears and a trim goatee that was probably as much facial hair as his boss was willing to accommodate in the 1970s, placed a disc on the turn-table. I snuck a glance at the album cover. It was *Dark Side of the Moon*. I turned up the volume and got a blast of sonic colours like a crayon box for my ears. I lowered the volume to a comfort zone and was able to pick out the vivid tangerine, carnation pink, orchid, sea green, cadet and cornflower blues, a palette of Van Gogh-like sounds and shapes I'd never known existed in a piece of music.

"Holy shit!" I said.

The salesman laughed and then put his finger to his lips.

I slipped off the phones.

"When you've got headphones on, you can't tell how loud you're speaking," he said.

I must have blanched.

"It's cool, man," he said. "Happens all the time."

I looked into the rest of the store. The family was en route, my father in the lead.

"Oops," I said.

The salesman ran interference. I placed the phones back on the tree branch and flipped the tag. A hundred and twenty. Never. I hadn't seen headphones advertised for that much in the circulars. I didn't know they existed. Oh, man.

The salesman must have sensed my dilemma. "That's the top-of-the-line model. You're not going to find better than that. But I know it's steep. Tell me what kind of range you're looking for and we'll come up with something."

"I've got $60," I said.

My father shot me a glance and then shook his head. Shaking didn't loosen the frown he wore.

The salesman said he had a perfect set of phones for $50 that produced similar sonic quality as the first set I'd tried but with a little less cushioning. I tried them. The Pink Floyd was just as pink and I was just as floored. I bought them.

"Never ever tell a salesman how much you've got," my father said on the way out of the mall. "They'll sell you overpriced crap you don't want."

I shrugged. "I want these."

"They'll end up like a Christmas present, used for a day then forgotten," my father predicted.

"That will be one day longer than he used any tool set you gave him," my mother said.

It was my father who forgot about them, except the first afternoon after work when he remarked how quiet it was down the hall. I wore my headphones on my bed as I did homework, as I wrote in my notebook, or just sat in my chair. I felt insulated, cut off from the outside world yet protected in the sound screen I'd created for myself. I felt as if I'd woken up in a log cabin set way back in the Mauricie national park after a two-foot drop of snow had buried every living creature and sound. I heard only what I wanted to hear, which was the icicle-clear notes of the music on my stereo. With some classical music I even tried to self-hypnotize myself on the floor, counting beats and trying to dig deeper and deeper into the music and into myself, seeking to dig into that snow-bank of sound. I woke when my sister kicked me in the side to get up for supper.

Sometime in November, CHOM announced it would play Queen's new album, *A Night at the Opera*, in its entirety, side one then side two, back to back, end to end, track to track, then repeat the cycle from 11 p.m. to 5 a.m. I plugged my phones in, lay on my back, and fell asleep to the rock'n'roll symphony in my ears. I heard the album twice before I crashed. Those times I tossed or turned or woke for a millisecond to flip my pillow I picked up snatches of song, tiny movements or notes from the '50s sci-fi skiffle "39," the motorized "I'm In Love With My Car" and the operatic "Bohemian Rhapsody." The next day bits of the tunes played back along with the curses of my father when he looked in my room in the morning: "What the fuck are you doing playing the radio all night?"

"What?" I'd said. "I wasn't bothering anyone. I had my headphones on!"

"Damn you and those blasted headphones! You don't play radios all night when you're sleeping!"

At the dinner table that night, my father said it was hard to communicate with me. I had my headphones on all the time. He said he felt I was ignoring him, that it was like talking into space. Of course he was exactly right.

"Don't smile at me like that, young man," he said. A drop of gravy fell onto the tablecloth from the fork he pointed at me.

"*Noël, regarde ta fourchette*," my mother said.

He put his fork on his plate. "I don't want you listening to those headphones all the time. I want you doing things. I want you doing your homework, or sweeping the stairs of snow."

"I already do those," I said.

"Don't answer me back like that," he said.

"Like what?" popped into my head. I didn't say it. I knew what he meant. Jerk.

Besides, even without my headphones, it was just as easy to ignore him, to let him talk into space. I could retreat into my insular world, made of equal parts solitude and anti-parental will, any time I wished. He made it so easy. The more he talked, the more I could imagine opportunities to escape in mounted snowdrifts.

A loud crash on the table awakened me from my reverie like a crack that precedes an avalanche. "Where does he go when I'm talking to him?" he said, to my mother presumably, but perhaps to no one.

"Are you listening to me?" He pointed at me. No fork. I nodded.

He put his hand down. He had large hands for a man his size, the skin tanned leathery brown and with burn marks from welding, made for work, with calloused palms the size of the abrasive wheel of a metal grinder and fingers like large rivets. When he grasped something — a hammer, a wrench, a beam, my upper arm — he didn't let go. Later, when he was dying, according to my sister, his hands would cling to the stainless steel side rail of the hospital bed and he would attempt to pull himself up to greet a visitor or to go to the toilet but though the grip on the rail was like glue, the muscles of his arms had atrophied and he would slump back into the bed.

I missed that point in his life, as I pretty much passed on his death. But not his funeral. I went to his funeral. As difficult, ignorant, verbally abusive and generally unloving as he was, still he was my father.

It had snowed lightly overnight, three inches at most, and, just before rush hour, the roads were still covered. Power lines and the lighter smaller tree branches genuflected under sugary snow. It hadn't snowed so much that I couldn't make out the models of some cars on Ste. Catherine Street by their outlines. The hearse outside St. Vincent de Paul was easy enough to identify. The side panels of the car, which was otherwise cleared of snow, displayed splashes from the drive to the church. I parked my car and crossed the street to the church on the corner. Holding the iron handrail, I walked up the dozen steps, cleared of snow yet wet, before reaching the plate-glass doors and the wrought-iron curlicue frame my father had fabricated. I pulled slowly and made no noise. I stood in the open space at the back of the pews. The service was already under way. I could see my mother in the aisle seat of the first pew, my sister and her husband in line next to her. My mother's black-gloved left hand lay on the edge of the pew, as if she were ready to turn about when she heard my footsteps up the aisle, or ready to dart out at the sound of a bell.

I slid into the last pew, and listened to the priest, a grey-haired, bespectacled man of medium height and exceptional girth, whose chasuble looked less like a priestly frock than a maternity dress.

"Noël and I became friends from the day when I took over as *curé* here," the priest said. "I remember standing at the pulpit, this one where I stand now, and saying the church was in debt, serious debt, and it would be up to the parishioners, some of you were there, you remember, it would be up to the flock to help the shepherd. After the mass, Noël approached me; he said, '*Mon père*, I haven't much money, but I have these two hands.' And he showed me his hands, lifted them like this" — and the priest brought up his open hands like the resurrected Christ, low, fingers pointed down. "And I noticed how the hands were calloused at the base of the fingers and near the thumb, and in the palm of his hands, tiny red marks. I knew this was a good man, and I said, 'Yes, Noël, my son. We will work together.' And together we went about the church repairing that which needed repairing. He designed and built the iron frame for our door. I imagine now," he said, with a wry, knowing smile, "he's working on repairing the Gates of Heaven.

"And when our days were done, Noël washed in the sacristy, took on a cassock and a surplice and helped me serve mass. His hands, as calloused and large as they were, were never so small and gentle as when handing me the chalice. Or when they formed a cup and he received communion.

"Truly, today we lose a strong, gentle and kind man. *Il était un bon homme.*"

I looked at the family in the front row. Though I'd met him only once or twice, I knew the man to be part of the family now, and I knew the woman next to him to be my sister, and next to them in the aisle seat the older woman — what did that mean, older? She was as old now as my grandmother was when I was born, yet this woman in the pew had no grandchildren, she had no white in her hair, she remembered what was worth remembering and could talk about these things lucidly — I knew her to be my mother. But who was this man the priest referred to? I knew that children's ideas of their parents and their parents' lives are very different from that of others. But had I gotten this completely wrong?

The priest ended his sermon, lifted the thurible and walked around the coffin. The gold container clanked against its chain as the priest raised and lowered it in a sign of the cross. Incense smoke rose heavily and slowly, like the priest himself. Its greyness was spiked through by the sun's rays as they crossed low in the room. The incense wafted to the back of the church, and followed me out the door.

The wind had picked up some, and I had to adjust my hat to keep it from blowing away. I got to my car, put the key into the door lock, and looked at my hands. Though I looked at them all the time — as a guitarist, how could I not — I'd stopped paying attention. I guess that happens. How large they were now. Light brown hair grew here and there over pale-olive skin. Though it was March and I had no tan, I could see where the skin colour faded in the indentation under my ring. I turned my hands over. My fingers were calloused, too, but from years of fretwork and there were signs of dry skin in the webbing from constant hand washing when I cooked.

I must have been 10 or 11 years old. My father and I were at a Canadian Tire store to buy a goalie's mitt for me. He handed me gloves to try on, but none fit. My hands were too small for the Major Junior-size mitts. We finally found one that fit and I went home proud of my new glove, anxious to get to the street to play with Marc and Norman and the gang of Choristes.

One evening in early November — it was near dark so it must have been about four-thirty — my mother called me in for dinner. I was the goalie, kick-saving tennis balls slap shot at me by some of the older kids on the street. I shouted that I wasn't hungry.

"*Rentre toute d'suite, avant que j'le dise à ton père.*"

The boys didn't stop shooting balls. I said, "In a minute."

"Now!" she screamed.

I obeyed, and ran to dinner.

Afterward, my father said he wanted to see how the glove was holding up and if it was moulding correctly. I swallowed hard. What had I done with the glove? I must have left it out, on top of the goal net in the street. I went outside, but the kids were gone. The net stood alone under the streetlight. The glove wasn't on top.

My father took me down to the basement that evening, where a few years but a lifetime before, we had made a Golden Gate, and had me clear an area about the size of a goal net. He placed me in front of the net and shot pucks that I caught in my bare hands.

Looking back at the parked hearse in front of the church, I turned the key, opened the door and got in the car. I put my hands up on the steering wheel and my head on my hands. I must have been there a while, when I heard a knock on the driver's side window. I looked up. It was an old man. I couldn't hear what he said, so I moved the lever that brought down the window. "*Tout va bien*?" he said.

"*Tout va bien*," I said.

"*Tout va bien*," he said, and his smile, just one short upward curl of a lip, and the way he tipped his hat and turned on his heel, was the coda I sought. I turned the ignition and set out.

Bridge
L'Espace entre les mots

"What might have been" and "what has been": synonyms of regret. What if my father hadn't lost his job and brought us to Quebec? What if Claude had finished his dinner before he'd left the table? What if the referendum had passed? What if Norman's uncle hadn't jumped? What if Louise and I had had sex as teenagers? What if what if what if. What if I had just called and talked to him or popped in when I knew which hospital he was in because my mother and sister had each phoned? "Call him," they said. "He wants to talk to you."

But how could I? I felt so coldly toward him I knew whatever words I spoke would be so brittle as to freeze on my tongue, crack under the pressure of enunciation. I would spit splinters of ice and watch them sting him and watch him bleed. And he would strike back with language as precise as an ice pick. Our relationship had frozen over and neither of us had the will to thaw it out.

"If you don't live it, it won't come out of your horn," Charlie Parker once said. After a particularly wounding fight, not long after I'd moved out, I went home, sat down and composed one of the angriest, most personal songs I've ever written. I banged on the deepest darkest chords my synthesizer and guitar could produce until the sun tried to break through the St. Laurent Blvd. smudge on my apartment windows. I slept until noon, got up and went to school, where I told my professors I wouldn't finish the term, drove down to the office of the security company and handed in my uniform. I was so fed up, that when my boss asked me why, I scowled. "*Chus tanné, hostie, comprends-tu?*"

I called the song "L'Espace entre les mots," and Bijou bought it.

"*C'est une chanson d'amour*," she said.

"*Maudit*," I said. "It's these people shouting at each other. They can't bear each other."

"*Non, non, non*," she said. "People who hate each other don't speak to each other like this. These people love each other; they just don't know how to express it."

"Well, thank you, I think. I'll remember the next time I speak to the asshole that I love him — and then I'll come up with some real juicy ways to express it."

Bijou laughed. It was an uncertain laugh, quickly suppressed. She knew then, even though we were still new together — in fact, neither of us had said the word "us" yet — that my relationship with my father was a source of some sadness and hurt. I hadn't said anything. Later, she invited me upstairs to her room where she showed me some new expressions of her own.

My obligation in writing "L'Espace entre les mots" was to myself first. It came from a source of pain and anger I clearly felt the need to deal with. Bijou and Patenaude, my psychologist, said my song had come out of the pain of love for my father. I don't know that I'd ever seen an expression of love from him. And I certainly didn't love *him*. I could never reconcile that supposed pain with what I wrote, just as I could never bridge the gap — never really wanted to bridge the gap — that divided my father and me. Some wounds, I believed, just don't heal. The screams and shouts continue although the source lies under six feet of topsoil with a limestone marker and not even exhumation will exorcise the ill spirits.

I had lived my life so differently than the way I wrote music.

A song begins with a note, one unwed note. I hear it, see it. I want to know more about it. Who is this note? Who are her folks? What's their outlook on life? Are they downers, or more upbeat? Who are their neighbours? When they invite friends over the house, who do they invite? The lone note in my head becomes a chord, which, from its first sounding, will create a mood, an emotion I try to exploit with chords related in tone or emotion. But to move between these chords, I need a bridge. The bridge is often my melody.

Writing the melody is where I test the elasticity of the chord, the give. Any one chord is a launch pad, a harmonic home base, a room to hang my hat, a six-and-a-half with an extra in the finished basement where I flop between girls. I take what I can from the chord and stretch it to meet the next chord. Wherever I go, I know I can — and must, actually — return to my chord home. Eleven o'clock curfew, you say? Yes, sir. But while we're out, limo driver, take us uptown, let's see what these notes can do. I elongate, I emphasize, I amplify, all the while compressing and condensing, narrowing here to broaden there. There's as much give and take in a melody as there are syllables in a dictionary. And that note, whatever I give to it and take from it, has one ultimate destination — to be reconciled with itself. To do that takes a bridge.

The day after Laurence had telephoned from Amsterdam, I had seen Jeanne to tell her the news. My grandmother hoped to see her *petite fille* Saturday.

"I thought Saturday was your day for church."

"Yes, yes, bring her before confession. We'll have time."

"Don't they call it something else now?" I said.

"Reconciliation," she said. "But sometimes I only remember the old word."

"I'm just happy she's coming home," I said. We were in the Residence St. Charles cafeteria for lunch. From our seats we could see outside, the leaves resplendent in their pre-Thanksgiving Day clothes. I told my grandmother about my mother's prayer, if that is the correct term, for safe flying. I said I would be holding the plane up for Laurence.

"We never went anywhere," Jeanne said.

"You, meaning?"

She had a piece of bread in her mouth. Crumbs fell from her lips into her plate, onto a sleeve, the tablecloth. "We, us," she said. "We didn't have time for vacations. On a farm, you know, always something to do and no money to spend on other things. Not like now."

"That's too bad."

Jeanne brushed off a bread crumb as she shook her head. "I wouldn't have wanted to travel with your father anyway."

"You mean my grandfather."

"*Quoi?*"

"I'm Michel. I'm your grandson. You remember that, right?"

"Have you had the soup? It always makes me burp."

"Me, too, Jeanne." The residence must have had a deal with the local grocer. Every time I had lunch with Jeanne, it was cream of broccoli.

"*Baptiste n'était pas un homme doux.*"

"I didn't know that."

"He was hard on your father. Your father was a gentle boy, very sweet. He always drew me flowers — since his father wouldn't let him pick them from the garden. Those were the ones we sold on the roadside along with the butter and sugar corn."

I had an image now of a man I didn't see as a boy. I'd never seen a photograph of him as a child. As far as I knew none existed. If the family didn't own a television until the late 1950s, it wouldn't have surprised me to discover they hadn't owned a camera until then either, by which point he had already left for the United States.

"That's a hard one for me to imagine, Jeanne. My father drawing pictures."

"We should have some dessert, don't you think, Michel? Can you get me the green one?"

I went back to the line, chose two bowls and returned to the table with the Jell-O.

"He always had a pencil and paper. Even in church, he drew pictures of the ceiling and the statues and the pillars. These beautiful, sweeping arches." Jeanne stopped, put her fist to her mouth and burped. "I was very upset with your mother, you know. Putting me in here."

"I know, Jeanne."

She ate her Jell-O. "I'm glad for you that Laurence is coming home."

"I think it will make Bijou very happy. She doesn't know yet. I haven't told her."

"It's a surprise?"

"Yes."

"Even the baby?"

"Not a baby anymore. He's two. But yes, a surprise."

"*T'es méchant.*"

"*Juste un peu.*"

"It's never too late," she said.

"For what, Jeanne? To get you out of here?"

"Here? Leave here? I don't want to leave here. All my friends are here. The ones who aren't dead. Besides, where else would I get soup like this?"

"Then what did you mean?"

"About what?"

"What did you mean, 'It's never too late'?"

"Laurence. It's never too late to start again, to say, 'I love you.' It's good that she called."

"Well, I think it might be too late for some people," I said.

"You know when Jesus says, 'Let the dead bury the dead'?"

I knew it. I had never understood it.

"It's OK. It's not too late for that either," she said. "When he says that, Jesus means the living go on living. We have to reconcile ourselves to ourselves, not to the dead. Leave the graveyard. Tend to your garden."

I must have looked at her blankly. Probably the way she sometimes looked at me.

"Your father's dead. What does it mean to him how you feel about him? Your relationship with him has plagued you all your life. It has affected people around you — what? Do you think Bijou hasn't told me? You don't need to reconcile with him. Reconcile yourself. Go home to your wife and be there for your daughter."

She held her arms out. I got up and grabbed her hands. They were cool and soft, the skin of her palms was thin yet loose, but her grip was tight and she rose from her seat easily. She took the handles of her walker, the front two legs had short ski-like feet and the back two had wheels. She skid-rolled to the elevator. Her room key hung from a Day-Glo yellow spring bracelet on her wrist.

"*Au revoir,* Michel," she said. "*Dis bonjour à Bijou et Laurence. Belle surprise.*"

I gave her a kiss. She had been such a stable influence in my life, never questioning, always encouraging — my first guitar, for crying out loud, in total defiance of my father! Jeanne got in the elevator and we waved, the door closed and, as she'd urged me, I turned my attention to Laurence. I imagined what she might look like. It had been almost 10 years. When Laurence left in her late teens, she still had adolescent down on her cheeks, arms and legs. Her smile, when we could manage to get one out of her, was full of white teeth and her eyes sparkled like the Lachine Rapids when the sun strikes the whitewater. Barcelona, Perpignan, Paris, Rome, Vienna, Ljubljana, Trieste, Dubrovnik. We didn't get postcards for the first year or so. Then a call, once, from Greece. We wired extra money and continued to feed an account she could withdraw from. Then no calls again for a while.

When she was 10 or so, we played a game, a board game, called Journey Through Europe, the object of which was, using a flight plan and dice, to move a figure across a dozen cities in Europe according to 12 cards picked out of a deck. The cards had historical and cultural information about the cities, places of interest and instructions on where to travel next — often involving diversions from one's flight plan. Laurence kept the instruction booklet by her side, and insisted that, as we worked our way through the deck of almost 200 cards, she read about cities we landed on. If a traveller approaches Bari from inland, he will pass through uninhabited terrain, miles of flat Trullian barrenness broken up by olive trees and small, round huts. A highlight of Hammerfest is its brightly painted

houses; tourists to this most northern of European cities are guaranteed daylight 24 hours a day from May to
September. A trip through Europe could read like a tour
for a B-list band, obscure or cities with musical names
but off the tourism trail: Galati, Larisa, Alicante, Biarritz,
Rovaniemi, Linz and back home.

One night a couple of years after Laurence left, Bijou
and I were sitting around the kitchen table with friends.
Had we heard from her? they asked. We had. She was
fine. What made her decide to go? another invitee asked.

"You know," I'd said, lying, "I don't think I remember
anymore."

I had glanced at Bijou afterward — just a check. She
had nodded and forced a smile. We both remembered.

With Laurence's return, a void would be filled. Yet, like
the truth about her father's identity, I was disposed to
believe another subject would be left undiscussed: the
events that preceded her departure. The child who wasn't.

Bijou had been adamant. Laurence was not old
enough to have a child.

"But the age of consent is 14, Maman," Laurence had
replied.

"Not in this house," said Bijou.

"That was four years ago!"

I wondered if Bijou remembered then that the young
woman she was fighting with had inspired "Premier Cri."

I think Laurence gave in because she had seen the
sense of it. But within a week of the abortion she was
gone. It was her most fitting Mosaic retaliation: a child
for a child.

When we saw Laurence at the turn of this new cen-
tury, I think we hoped that we could turn over our rela-

tionship, too. Bijou had another weeklong engagement in Paris in May and we spent a month afterward in Séguret, a flowery village near the Dentelles, full of old houses and window shutters, student painters and postcard makers. We invited her to the house we had rented. We'd set up a room just for her. We'd talked about almost nothing else. We were seeing Laurence again! I could sense in Bijou a break in the clouds that hung over her, noticed it even when she'd been on stage — her between-song chatter was chipper and the selection of songs optimistic. Instead, Laurence preferred a neutral area, a café in Avignon near where she lived and worked as a guide at the papal palace.

She sipped her espresso and picked at a chip in the plate.

Laurence had not grown in height. She seemed thinner. We said so. She shrugged.

"Have you been eating well?"

"Yeah, it's fine; it's France."

She could hardly make eye contact. We could see the fatigue in them, though not the kind of exhaustion that dulled and emptied them by too many experiences she didn't want to talk about. Her hair was longer.

I asked if she remembered Journey Through Europe, if she had ever made it to those cities from the board.

She looked up. "You remember that?" She smiled. "That was so much fun. I used to hog all the cards so I could read all the info, like a tour guide. And you, you never seemed to be able to get out of Catania or some place like that. We—" She stopped.

"We want you to come home," Bijou said at last. She reached to touch her daughter.

Laurence pulled her hand away. "I can't," she said. "Not yet."

"When?" I asked.

The shake of her head was slight. She slid out of her chair and left.

When Laurence called last week, I'd wanted to ask, but didn't and now didn't think I ever would: Why? Why had she stayed away so long after we'd met in Avignon? Why couldn't she have called more often? But at least she was coming back.

Chorus

Pourquoi non, moi et toi

I looked at the Molson clock. There would now be no time to get to Papineau; that errand would have to wait. But with traffic edging forward I would have just enough time to make it to Trudeau to pick up Laurence. I looked out the window. Incredibly, slowly, I had somehow managed to move parallel to the Ferris wheel of La Ronde. Beyond it and above it and in front of me were the Olympic Stadium — I couldn't imagine what my old man would have said at the final cost; Télé-Québec, where Bijou once recorded a Christmas show (a video showed up on YouTube last year); a number of anonymous towers, and the twin peaks of St. Vincent de Paul Church, put up for sale as condo units, the rectory now the home of the Word for Life Church. We were slow accelerating off the bridge. I shut off the car radio and lowered the window. As I passed one of the span's main girders, I heard a loud clang. I turned and tried to locate its source. Maybe it was a rock spit up from a truck tire that struck a piece of metal. The sound resonated. I'd heard the tone before, and not just the tone, but a resemblance in its timbre. It had surprised me then as well.

We had decided — *he* had decided — that the family would have an "island vacation" that summer. He didn't mean the Mediterranean or the Aegean or the South Pacific. Nor Jamaica, nor Guadeloupe. Father meant Montreal. We were short of funds for a summer vacation that would take us off the island, so that summer — the summer I turned 15, the summer of April Wine's "You Won't Dance With Me" and "Chaque jour qu'on approche la mort," from Beaupré's latest — my father stated the

235

two weeks of the construction holiday would be *chez nous,* a Montreal "island vacation," complete with the Jacques Cartier Bridge, the Victoria Bridge, the Champlain Bridge, the Mercier Bridge, and those bridges everyone's crossed at some point in their Montreal lives but has never known the names of: the one to Île Perrot, the one to Vaudreuil, the ones that go to Laval, and to Repentigny. And that little one that crosses to Île Ste. Hélène. My mother, no longer trapped by my father and his ideas of family vacations, stuck inside the car somewhere in New England, or northern or southern Quebec, begged off the bridge hunt. She took my sister along with her and they swam every day at the recently opened neighbourhood pool and went to the library where they joined a summer reading club.

I didn't take my notebook that year, but I did learn that, before the Honoré-Mercier was erected in 1934, commuters to Montreal from Kahnawake or Châteauguay had to take a ferry. Apparently, there's a sidewalk on the bridge, too, but only a nutcase would take it, I thought. Before the Victoria Bridge opened in 1859, there was no way to cross the St. Lawrence River between the Thousand Islands and the Gaspé Peninsula that did not involve getting wet or dodging ice floes. Then, once they'd built the truss and caused a growth spurt in the Montreal economy, it would have been foolhardy of our forefathers not to imagine building more modes of traversing the river. At five kilometres long and with 24 icebreaker piers, it was the longest bridge in the world at construction. The Champlain, the newest of the four bridges, had the advantage of the latest technology, prestressed concrete over the entire nine miles of the complex. It opened in 1962, four years after announcement of the project and named in honour of the 350th anniversary of Samuel de Champlain's arrival in Quebec. My father's monologues went on for a lot longer than this, were much more detailed in terms of span lengths and heights and types of steel used and only once did I answer a question right, when my father asked, "What type of bridge is the Jacques Cartier?" and I was able to answer, "Steel truss cantilever."

"And what is a 'steel truss cantilever'?" he asked.

We were on the sidewalk in the middle of the centre span (334 metres) of the bridge. It was an exceptionally blue July day. The air felt light and crisp and I could hear the laughter and shouts of children at La Ronde below us. I could have been there with Norman.

"I don't know," I murmured.

"I don't know. I don't know. Are you not listening when I talk to you? It's like you got those headphones on even when you don't." He shook his head and turned from me. He started to walk and I followed.

"The Jacques Cartier Bridge was modelled after the Quebec Bridge, which had been built eight years before the design concept for this one was approved. The Story Bridge in Brisbane, Australia, was a copy of this one. It was originally named the Pont du Havre, but four years after opening, it was renamed to honour the great adventurer's first trip up the St. Lawrence River."

I wanted to block his didacticism out but feared another question. I knew he would. He would have to. He would ask the question, whatever the question was, and expect me to not know the answer. Whatever the task, he expected me to louse it up. It would infuriate him and, perversely, it would please him, too. I was no challenge to him.

"The original design called for a tramway to be built beside the roadway," he said, stopping again and turning in toward the bridge. He leaned against the guardrail. "But, as you see, the tramway was never built and, instead, an extra lane of car traffic was allowed each way, which was a lucky thing. There are now 43 million vehicle crossings of this bridge annually. This would make the Jacques Cartier the second or first busiest bridge in Canada?"

"First," I said without hesitation.

"Second," he said.

Please don't ask me, please don't ask me.

He picked up a rod of metal about a quarter of an inch round that he found on the sidewalk. "Michel, what do you really expect to do with yourself in two, three years' time?"

I was about to shrug, but he didn't wait for an answer.

"I know you're into your music now and you're into the girls and you read a lot, and I suspect you're probably into the beer and the cigarettes like others your age, but where is all that going to get you? What can you do with a book? What can you do with a guitar? Better for you to do as I did and pick up a trade. I know right now your thumbs get in the way — all 10 of them — but you can learn a trade. You don't have to follow in my footsteps exactly. You can go to school to learn how to be an electrician or a plumber. You can—"

"Pa, I can't be an electrician or a plumber. That involves stuff I don't know anything about."

"But that's what I'm saying, you can still learn that."

We faced each other. I could hear the shouts and clamour from the amusement park between the whoosh of the passing cars.

"I don't *want* to learn it. I want to go to school to learn how to compose music."

How could I tell this man how central music and words — three chords, really, and a rhyming diction-ary — had become to my life, how they'd displaced him as the bridge to my American past, my Quebec present and whatever lay beyond that? Three chords were the tools for how I planned to build my future, not hammers and nails and circular saws.

"You are *not* going to school to learn how to write songs."

"Pa, you can't keep me from doing what I want."

I could see I had neared a dangerous spot. I was close to pissing him off so royally he might have struck me right there on the bridge, but worse than that, much more injurious, I had, without having said the words, told him I had no intention of being like him. I can't now imagine, 30 years later, what that must have felt like. I had told him he was not worth emulating. I had severed the line that connected son to man for 400 years in Que-bec. I could hear it break like a snapped guitar string.

He slammed the metal rod against the guard rail. An angry, high tone rose from the metal. I could hear the range in the frequency; I could feel it in my chest, the way I felt my own anger and could sense my father's. The frequency slowed and the tone lowered and then it was gone. I stood stunned by my father's outburst, and mes-merized by the sound it had produced. I saw a bolt on the ground — six inches long and about half an inch thick — my father would probably have called it five-eighths — and I picked it up. I struck the guardrail, too. The sound differed from my father's. It was lower, slower, a brown tone versus the redder sound he'd produced.

I could not say what my father thought at that moment. I had answered his anger in a way he probably had not expected, had challenged him to respond in a way he hadn't anticipated. I hadn't, this time, failed him. And he did not fail me. He took his piece of metal and rapped it against the inside of the I-beam to his right. It gonged like a church bell. I responded by resonating the spindles between the guardrail and the parapet like a one-handed marimba player. My father flogged the flanges of another beam. I struck the rail again, this time with the head of the bolt. Soon we were running up and down the sidewalk tapping, thrashing, whipping, pelting, battering, pounding every part of the bridge we could reach with any tool we could pick up off the sidewalk. We played the bridge in this way for a quarter-of-an-hour until a Sûreté du Québec officer stopped, and asked us to move on.

Fin

Songwriter Michel Laflamme is stuck in rush-hour traffic on the Jacques Cartier Bridge in Montreal. While waiting for police and firefighters to try to talk down a potential suicide, Michel turns on the radio and hears his wife, Bijou, founding member of Beaupré, the seminal Quebec folk-rock group. The music takes Michel across a thirty-year span of memory, through the emotional and political upheavals of his own life and that of his Belle Province.

Jack Kerouac meets Beau Dommage! This novel of a coming-of-age in the Montreal music scene of the Seventies is a Québécois blues, wise, pungent, and funny.
— **Peter Behrens** (Governor-General's Award winning author of *The Law of Dreams*)

A former senior editor at *The Montreal Gazette*, Raymond Beauchemin is the author of *Salut! The Quebec Microbrewery Beer Cookbook* and editor of several anthologies of Quebec literature in English. He has taught creative writing and international journalism at Concordia University in Montreal. A Massachusetts native, he has lived and worked in Abu Dhabi and currently lives in Ontario. He is married to the writer Denise Roig.